Black Angel Book One

Also by Dolores Maria Davis:

Black Angel Book Two
and
Harem Twins, a trilogy

The characters and story are fictional.

Cover design by Quincy Macklin

Edited by Ming the Merciless

Readied for Publication by Nic Wainwright

Black Angel Book One
Dolores Maria Davis
www.DoloresMariaDavis.com

Printed in the United States of America
ISBN 978-0-9976240-1-4

10 9 8 7 6 5 4 3 2 1

Dedication

This book is dedicated to Nic Wainwright

This story is written as a result of a tour I took through a grand house in Montecito, California many years ago. I wish to thank the Palos Verdes Library Writers Group for listening to and critiquing my work.

Black Angel Book One

Chapter 1

Magdalena D'Alessandro arrived early to remove the card from the extravagant wreath that lay on Angelina's casket. She read the sentiment, then placed it in her purse, knowing it would anger her father that 'The Organization' had sent flowers to her younger sister's funeral. His fragile health needed no additional shock. Taking a front row seat on an uncomfortable folding chair next to her father, Magdalena could only guess about the arrangements for the Catholic services.

Her father had not included her in planning her sister's funeral. In this small Westwood, California cemetery, attendants had partitioned off an area along a wall of crypts, then set up rows of chairs to create a temporary chapel. Magdalena sat looking up at the huge photograph of her sister that stood beside the casket. In the photo, she looked like royalty, seated on her $20,000 mount, Immigrant Song. Saddened, Magdalena looked away from the imposing photo and up at the wall of crypts. Near the ceiling an ornate bronze door hung open at an empty crypt. She gathered Papa wanted Angie to be laid to rest in grandeur. Near the casket, a small bronze plaque, ultimately destined to mark the crypt noted her short life: Angelina D'Alesandro 1965-1983. Magdalena slipped off her glasses, now splattered with tears from her eyelashes and looked at her father.

Dominic D'Alessandro had insisted Angie be interred in this hidden and iconic cemetery where many of Hollywood's elite were buried. After the chapel filled, a priest entered in a white simple robe to say Mass, assisted by a pair of Alter boys. A long droning homily followed the Gospel. Dominic's hand trembled and his face ran with tears. Magdalena worried that he might sink into another stroke. After his first episode, she was told by his doctor to keep him quiet and away from emotional events. His doctor didn't know that she and Dominic rarely spoke anymore.

When the Mass ended, everyone seemed to be holding their breath as people awaited the final grimness. The men and women all looked up. *How often was someone encrypted, and was that even the term?* A mechanical groan came from the large hoist that held Angie's coffin, and hadn't seemed evident earlier, now rose to the dark opening above. The device stopped with a jerk like an ill-controlled robot. A wrenching screech from the casket being pushed into the abyss unsettled the crowd. When the bronze door shut, the harsh sound sent the final message that vivacious, talented and high-spirited Angie was entombed.

By the end of the service, crying and sobbing sounds were heard from both men and women. Magdalena couldn't remember when she had last cried, having learned long ago to stifle tears but bile continued up her digestive track. Swallowing hard, and for diversion, she turned to see who had come. She had no idea who had been notified of her sister's death, as her father had not included her in the funeral arrangements. She found him increasingly hostile toward her after overhearing her conversation with Jimmy Sciacca. When she told Sciacca that she would be taking over her father's legal practice.

After that, she felt her father had closed a chapter on their lives. *I pray to God Papa's scorn for me will one day end.*

She swiveled to look at their household help seated in the row behind her. Gino, the groundskeeper and his sister Maria, the cook cried uncontrollably. Of all the help, she had been closest to Angie. From the time Angie was seven-years-old, she and Maria had spent hours in the kitchen together, baking biscotti and Angie's favorite chocolate chip cookies. Looking back, Maria had been a surrogate mother to Angie. Knowing her well, Maria protested that Angie was too young and reckless to go to Hawaii, where she met her mysterious death! *But Angie had begged Papa to go and, as usual, got her way.*

Magdalena reached back and clutched Maria's hand. The cook looked at her and tried to smile. Gino's hand covered theirs without a word turning his face away.

Magdalena nodded to Alberto, her father's aide, and his spouse, Rosella, the housekeeper. They sat in silence. *Alberto is such a loyal aide to Papa. God must have sent him.*

Magdalena caught the eyes of Angie's equestrian trainer, several of her riding mates and their parents, all with tear stained faces. Sitting alone, tanned and tow-headed, was Lance, her father's first physical therapist, and her first date. They exchanged polite nods. Farther back sat Jimmy Sciacca, the Organization's Boss with Joseph Cozza and his brother Vinnie, trusted subordinates. She would thank them for flying in from Las Vegas as soon as they were out of her father's view.

Magdalena rose and turned to Alberto, "Please drive my father and the family home." She indicated to the staff whom she now referred to as family. It seemed appropriate, since they were like a surrogate family for her and her father, the only ones left in the big house. She kissed her father on his forehead. He frowned, his face pale with grief. Looking straight ahead, her father engaged the switch on his electric wheelchair to exit down the aisle, with Alberto following him out to the car.

Walking toward the back of the chapel, Magdalena released a long sigh. Trying to cope with her father's rejection knowing that the limited love they once shared was gone, devastated her. This blow, coupled with managing the detritus of Angelina's affairs, had worn her thin. Her father had arranged for the funeral, using his private investigator, Harold. She was left with the Hawaiian police report and death certificate, Angie's belongings, her horses, and her personal effects. She also knew she had to move forward with plans to become the family provider. After her father's last stroke, he could no longer practice law. In that recent telephone conversation with Sciacca, she had to explain that sad fact. Now she must represent clients of the Organization, as Magdalena had begun to refer to the Mafia Family.

At the back of the chapel, she approached Sciacca, who embraced her. "What can I do for my goddaughter? I am so sorry you have lost your only sister." Magdalena nearly broke into tears at his fatherly embrace, something she hadn't experienced in years. "That's kind of you Mr. Sciacca. I'm sure time will help," was all she could think to say.

She turned to handsomely groomed Joseph Cozza standing attentively, palms extended allowing her to come to him. She put her hands on his chest, leaned close to him and whispered in his ear. "Meet me at the Bel Air for dinner at eight. Make reservations for a table and a room for the night."

Sciacca's hand rose to suppress a smile at her newfound intimacy with Joseph. Suddenly Joseph looked as though he was attending a wedding, not a funeral.

*****

Magdalena stepped into her 1973 Jaguar XKE, a car Sciacca had arranged she receive on her eighteenth birthday. Sciacca had wanted Magdalena to have a car on her birthday for two reasons. She was a beautiful Italian girl, and never noticed by her father. He had tried to make it look as though Magdalena's father had given her the car, but he hadn't. D'Alessandro was infuriated by the gift, and it remained an ugly reminder that he had forgotten her birthday that year. He was never able to condone such an extravagant gift or acknowledge it, some five years later.

At breakneck speed, Magdalena raced up Stone Canyon to their Holmby Hills residence. She would have a long swim in the indoor pool at the villa, where she could find answers to all her problems.

Dominic D'Alessandro had negotiated this villa as part of his salary when he in desperation took the position of counsel to the southern California Mafia. Severe medical debt and the necessity to raise two young daughters forced his decision, but he never forgave himself. She had been fourteen and Angelina seven-years old. Magdalena knew his decision shattered his self-esteem.

Magdalena's back stiffened as she sped up winding Stone Canyon road. *Angie, I will go to Hawaii and if I find any reason to avenge your death, I will.*

Once at home in the pool, Magdalena swam her usual laps, therapy her doctor had prescribed years earlier. Swimming, she reminisced when she and her sister were young…

Chapter 2

"Shush," Magdalena whispered standing barefoot in her nightgown on the cold kitchen linoleum, "I want to listen to Papa, he's in the front room talking to men dressed up in suits." Magdalena strained to peek around the corner, keeping her seven-year old sister Angelina back with her arm.

"Why are they yelling?" asked Angelina, chewing on one of her blonde braids.

"I'm not sure, but I think it has something to do with moving away." As she said moving away, Magdalena grimaced.

"But we just moved to grandma and grandpas!" Now do we have to leave here too!" Angelina said softly, tears starting. "Is this because mama died?"

"Don't cry, Angelina, you'll wake grandma and grandpa," Magdalena said, putting an arm around her little sister as she guided her back to their bed. "You go back to sleep, and we can talk in the morning."

Once Angelina was in bed, Magdalena went back to continue listening to her father and the men. "Only my friends call me 'Del.' To you, I'm Dominic D'Alessandro" Magdalena heard her father shout when she returned.

A chair creaked as one of the men in the living room stood. "Think about it D'Alessandro." She heard her father shuffle them out the door and slam it behind them.

Magdalena had seen those same men when they came to see her father earlier in the month. They had an angry conversation then, too, she remembered. Peeking into the living room, she saw her father make up his bed on the couch with tight jaws and lips.

Quietly, Magdalena limped toward the small sunroom that sufficed as a sleeping place for herself and Angelina. Her grandparents slept in the only real bedroom in their small flat. On her way, she noticed a stack of opened mail on the kitchen table. Earlier she'd seen her father writing items on of his yellow tablets. Sure he was in bed Magdalena reviewed the list: Dozens of doctor bills from her mother's cancer, charges from the clinic for her own polio, a six month-old cemetery bill shocked her. Now she understood why they were living in their grandparent's one bedroom flat.

Papa must not make a big enough salary as a district attorney to pay all these bills. I guess we are out of money. Living in Little Italy sounds pretty, but it isn't. Our old house was much nicer. And there, we didn't have to take a bus to Catholic school.

Magdalena tiptoed back to the sunroom, trying not to wake her sister. She brushed her long black hair and quickly formed a single braid then knelt at her bedside and whispered her prayers before slipping into the bed she and Angelina shared. Her last thoughts were: *'Dear Mary, Mother of God, please help me to always care for Papa and Angelina. Mama would have wanted this to be. The public pool is six blocks away. I'll get up early and walk there, come back and get Angie off to school, just like Mama used to. Grandma is too old to help so I'll braid Angie's hair and see that her uniform is pressed. Then I'll just have enough time to catch the bus to Saint Augustine's.'*

Fading into sleep, Magdalena knew she would always take care of her ten-year-old sister and her father. Her young age and having had polio were not going to alter that.

No one was supposed to get the disease in 1970, but a wave of dreaded polio-myelitis had returned and struck people, mostly the young. The doctor told her father swimming was the best therapy. He also had said that one of her legs would remain shorter than the other.

*****

Sitting at the kitchen table, Papa looked tired. Magdalena saw gloom on her grandparent's faces, too. Something was wrong, and Magdalena thought she knew only part of the problem.

Magdalena's grandfather put down his fork and said, "Dominic, you tell the girls. They need to know,"

Her father wiped his mouth with a paper napkin, and pushed his chair away from the table. When he stood, Del heaved his barrel chest and straightened his broad shoulders. "We are moving, but to a nice place, so don't feel bad. He quickly added, and grandma and grandpa are coming with us."

Angelina cried out in distress. "We are leaving 'Little Italy' too!"

"Yes, we are Angelina, but…

Sobbing, Angelina ran to the sun porch to collapse on the bed.

Magdalena reached for her father's hand. "Papa, if we are moving to a better place, why are you so sad?"

The grandparents exchanged grim glances.

"Would you like to go for a walk with me, my *figlia,* daughter?"

Magdalena nodded, and went to get her sweater.

*****

The incoming San Francisco fog veiled the sun. Magdalena and her father walked in dense cloudiness that didn't keep the kids from play. A rank odor filled Magdalena's nostrils when they passed the battered garbage cans that lined the sidewalks. They waved back at the local barber as he locked up his shop for the evening. They took a turn down an alley, away from the noisy children playing games in the street.

Looking straight ahead, her father spoke without emotion. "Magdalena, you know I've worked as a prosecutor for twenty years in the federal courts, don't you?"

"Yes, Papa."

"Well, when we move, I am going to become a defender in the county courts."

"But you have always prosecuted the criminals: illegal traffickers of guns, alcohol, cigarettes and stuff like that."

"You know a lot for your fifteen years, *figlia mia,*" Del said turning to look at her.

"Of course, I do. I am going to be a lawyer just like you, and graduate in the top of my class at USF, like you did.

Del took a large handkerchief from his pocket. Magdalena watched him wipe his eyes and blow his nose.

Magdalena looked down trying to minimize her limp. "You're going to work for those guys in the 'garbage business,' aren't you, Papa?"

Del's shoulders dropped. "No, these are a different bunch. The same..." Del hesitated. He couldn't tell his daughter that he had negotiated a deal with a Los Angeles family. "The same business but a company in southern California. But how did you know that?"

Magdalena looked beneath his bushy eyebrows into his sad black eyes. "It's all those doctor bills, isn't it, Papa?"

"Yes, it's all those doctor bills," he said putting his arm around his daughter.

Magdalena felt her father's pain and realized that she had guessed right about his decision to work for the men in expensive suits. "Where are we moving, Papa?" Magdalena said, never doubting her father's decisions.

"To a small part of Los Angeles called Holmby Hills."

"Is that where you will practice, Papa?"

"No, I will go into the Los Angeles courts. I understand it is about a thirty-minute drive to downtown L.A."

She watched her father trying to look positive, straightened his posture. "And I must tell you that a large, beautiful house, has been arranged for us. I'm told it is a Mediterranean styled villa," he said, looking as though he was trying to form the words with enthusiasm.

The bosses D'Alessandro negotiating with knew how expensive the area was. But they wanted a nearby hotel for meetings from time to time, and the Bel Air Hotel sat just below residential Holmby Hills. It was hard to bug a hotel. And, D'Alessandro had vehemently refused their offer unless a house was included. Finally, with an understanding that D'Alessandro would make monthly payments, they told him a down payment would be made to secure the residence. He even got them to provide some of the muscle to help him move. He had chosen a grand, expensive villa. In due time, D'Alessandro would devise a devious plan whereby the gangsters he was about to represent would pay for his home.

Magdalena and her father walked in silence for a block or more when Magdalena turned to him. "So now you can pay all those doctor bills and Mama's funeral costs."

Nodding, her father pulled Magdalena close as they continued to walk. "And, let's keep this from Angelina. It would be too hard on her. She is like her mother, more delicate than you."

Magdalena didn't think her sister was delicate, but she didn't want to disagree with him, especially now. Then with an astute observation for her young years, Magdalena added, "Mama would have said that a 'black angel' has come to us."

Chapter 3

Paola Mancuso, Del's sister, was a childlike woman happiest around young people. She showed her adoration for her nieces by arriving with gifts for birthdays and holidays. Once, the family had a large suburban home and she would stay for weekends. No one knew when she would arrive or how long she would stay. She couldn't be reached by phone, and it was never clear where she was living. Paola seemed to come and go like a gypsy, a simple but lively woman in her mid-thirties. Magdalena remembered that Papa had to go to the police station and bring Paola home more than once, and she was never quite sure why.

By accident, Paola had come to visit on moving day. A truck piled high with the humble possessions of the D'Alessandro households sat in front of the apartment. When Paola saw the truck and the moving men, she covered her mouth, raced the steps to the second floor, "*Mio Dio*!" she said to Del, who was heading out of the apartment with a box of law books.

"Hello, Paola. We're moving. We've taken a house in Holmby Hills, and Mama and Papa are coming with us," he said bluntly.

"Is that in this country?" she asked wide-eyed.

"Yes, Paola, it is in this country. Pick up one of those

boxes if you want to help." When Angelina saw her aunt, she went running, arms outstretched. "*Zia*, we are moving again. Oh, come with us, please?"

As Paola lifted Angelina and swung her in a circle, she called, "*Mi Nipote*, tell me where is this place you are going?"

Carrying an armful of clothing, Magdalena went to her aunt. "We are moving to Holmby Hills, Aunt Paola. Papa is going to practice law in Los Angeles," Magdalena said, as she set down the garments and hugged her aunt.

"You'll come with us, won't you, *Zia*?" Angelina again begged. Paola could be witless, but it was with an interested eye that she viewed the men loading the furniture.

*****

Angelina, nestled between Magdalena and her grandmother, had fallen asleep with her head on Magdalena's shoulder in the back seat of the family Corvair. At first it looked like they were off the main road and lost, but her father had driven between two pillars, bearing massive wrought iron gates with the right address. "Are you sure this is the right place, Dominic?" asked Magdalena's grandmother.

Having learned about this home through a real estate agent, as opposed to viewing the property himself, D'Alessandro looked somewhat unsure. "The address is correct," said Del, as they wound up the long driveway. "This must be it."

Magdalena's grandfather followed them in the small truck with the household goods.

The drive was lined with mature shrubbery, and when her father rolled down the car window, Magdalena could smell the cool evening air scented with the white blossoms of large bushes that lined the drive. Next, she could feel the car passing over gravel. She would later learn that this area was referred to as a parking court. It covered the ground in front of the Mediterranean two-story house.

Both vehicles came to a halt. A man with a flashlight, a wad of keys, a realtor, waited for them. He explained he would return in the morning to give them a tour of the property. He went on to say the gas, electricity and phones had been turned on. He handed Del's mother a large fruit basket and left. It was too late to explore the rest of the house with its many rooms.

Having made the drive from San Francisco, everyone was too exhausted from an entire day on the road to unpack the truck. With makeshift arrangements for beds, they settled in a cozy den downstairs. Magdalena could see there were some beautiful pieces of furniture that had been left behind in the house. Magdalena, Angelina and Paola chose the floor on a richly colored oriental rug. Grandma's quilts came in handy for their beds. She watched her father settle into a chair that reclined. Grandma and grandpa were offered the large leather couch for their bed. Before Magdalena settled herself to sleep, she kissed her father on his head. "Thank you, Papa, for such a beautiful house."

*****

A melodic chime sounded the next morning puzzling everyone. Her father rose from his chair to reach for his wrinkled windbreaker. "It's the doorbell; I'll get it," he said, clearing his throat.

The front door opened into a glass-enclosed room about six-feet square, surrounded by ornate ironwork. An exterior anti-room like this, in the East, kept out bad weather. Here, in L.A., the sunlight warmed the room and potted orchids lined the tile floor.

"What do you want?" Del asked in a rough voice,

peering through the opened mahogany door and choosing not to step into the outdoor glass room.

The two Cozza brothers stood there in shiny suits and silk shirts, with narrow ties and greased hair. "It's not what we want; it's what you want, *Signore*," Joey, the older brother said, holding one palm open. Vinnie added, "You know, like we could get you some donuts and coffee. Maybe some milk for the girls."

"No! What I want is that you don't show up here at…, Del looked at his watch, …at 7:30 on a Saturday morning.

"We just came to…"

"Leave," Del interrupted, "I need to get some groceries for my family." He walked away, slamming the heavy mahogany door. It sounded as though a bomb had dropped.

As the Cozza's were getting into their Toronado, Vinnie said, "What a prick."

"He's a hot shot lawyer; what do you want?" Joey said, shrugging.

An hour later, the brothers returned to place four bags of groceries at the front door. They then called on Gino an aging caretaker that had lived in a small shack on the property for twenty years. Gino, nervously took some instructions from the brothers, who handed him an envelope containing two thousand dollars, and a map of the Bel Air Holmby Hills area. For the first time in twenty years there the caretaker stood cap in hand, calling at the front door of the house, instead of the service entrance.

*****

Paola had been up early and climbed the stairs to find four bedrooms on the east side of the house, one with a fireplace, all with private bathrooms. She returned to cuddle on the floor with her niece.

"Should we find the kitchen sink and wash our faces,

Paola?" Sleepy-eyed Angelina asked her cousin.

"Angelina, never again will you have to wash your face in the kitchen sink in this house."

One by one the family awoke, ready to explore their grand new home. "Come on," said Del, "Let's see what this old house has to offer." Leaving the den, they all inspected the spacious foyer by daylight, its floor laid with black and white marble squares. Magdalena watched Angelina and Paola go up the side staircase to the bedrooms, two steps at a time. Grandma and grandpa stood mesmerized by the scale of the interior looking unsure where to go next. Magdalena took her father's hand to find a formal dining room off the foyer, with another door leading to the butler's pantry and a huge kitchen. "Papa, let's go back to the entrance, I thought I saw a library there last night." Magdalena took her father's hand to return to the west end of the house where there was a large library with a sunny patio. "This is a beautiful room, Papa. Wouldn't you like to make this your office?" She watched as her father nodded, sighed and leaned against the doorframe to view the craftsmanship of the elegant fruitwood cabinets.

"This is a workplace for a baron," he said.

"Just think Papa you can fill the shelves with your law books, and your Roman history books. Magdalena took her father's hand. "Come on Papa, there is even more to see. They shook their heads in amazement when they passed a small room the size of a closet for just the telephone. Together, they continued to investigate the grand house. Magdalena found a door with knobs on it. Papa, how do you open this door? Del smiled, 'There's a button on the wall over there. Push it. "When Magdalena reached over and pressed the black plaster button, the door slid to one side. "It's an elevator!" She cried, I didn't know houses had elevators.

"Get in. Get in." They entered the small, lighted elevator car.

"Now what! Magdalena said. Which button do we push? One or two?"

"Neither, for now. Push the one that says 'P.'' She pressed the 'P' and the door slid closed, making her nervous. The car jerked then slowly descended. When the car noticeably slowed, Del told Magdalena, "Quick! Close your eyes until I tell you to open them."

Magdalena complied just as the elevator bumped to a stop. She heard the door slide open and through her closed eyelids saw lights come on. Many lights. She took a deep breath and smelled something familiar. What is that? She wondered. Chemicals?

Okay, open your eyes now," his voice echoing from the room beyond. She put the echo together with the odor and knew in an instant what she would see. The opened her eyes.

"Oh, Papa! It's a pool!"

"Yes, it's a pool. The doctor said it might help your legs."

"Oh, Papa, I am so happy!" She put her arms around him and squeezed hard.

Del stroked her hair and smiled at her. Then his expression became serious, his eyes looking straight into hers. "*Mia bambina*, never let this memory get old. Remember this moment forever."

"I will, Papa, I will." And she did remember this, the brightest moment of her childhood, always.

"Papa, the whole room is lined in beautiful tiles."

"Yes, it is, *mi figlia*. I was told it was just refurbished. And it is all yours. Here you can become a little fish, a

Pescolina."

She hugged him again, as he searched for his handkerchief to blow his nose. When they arrived back on the ground floor, Magdalena was overwhelmed with the fairytale house - the pool, the landscaping. "This house should be in a movie, or maybe it has been," she whispered to herself.

"Well, I'm hungry," called Del, "Shall we go out to breakfast somewhere, everybody?" But before anyone could answer, the doorbell chimed.

Not wanting to see the Cozza brothers again, Del set his jaw and grimaced as he went to the door, and flung it open. "What the hell are you two…but the Cozza's were not there.

It was a small stocky man with stooped shoulders, who stood twisting his cap in his hands. "*Buongiorno*, *Signore* D'Alessandro. I am Gino, the caretaker. I was told deliver this," he said in broken English as he handed Del an envelope and indicated four bags of groceries.

Del extended his hand to the stooped man. This countryman resembled family and friends he'd grow up with.

Magdalena watched as the two men began a lively conversation in Italian. It wasn't long before they wandered off together, breakfast forgotten. Both men were barrel chested and broad shouldered, but Gino was the shorter. From the rear, they looked like they could be brothers.

Chapter 4

Magdalena knew deep down her father resented working for the men in the garbage business. But this house was so grand, the pool so big, and the property so beautiful, how could Papa not want to live here? And the little Italian caretaker, Gino, made it perfect. Magdalena sighed and joined her grandparents.

Grandma and grandpa had found their way to the butler's pantry. "Is this the kitchen?" Grandfather asked when Magdalena entered. She looked around. "I don't see an oven. Maybe in this, she pointed at the swinging door with the circular window. On the other side of the door they found an immense old-world cooking room. Pot racks held large copper cauldrons. Two commercial stoves stood ready to accommodate any size event, and a double door refrigerator on high legs resembled a small car. The walk-in chill room with an old- fashioned latch could deep a big family for a year.

Magdalena saw her grandmother halt then back out of the kitchen, her eyes wild with fright. Magdalena followed her when she ran screaming to the front door. "Dominic, this is a *maligno*, evil place. I cannot stay here. Take me home to 'Little Italy,' her grandmother cried. Del ran to his mother's side. "Mama, what is it?" By then, the screams had brought everyone to the door. Magdalena's grandmother paid no attention to them, but headed toward the truck, still piled high with their family belongings. As her panic grew, she ran so rapidly she stumbled on the gravel and nearly fell.

Magdalena saw her father run to his mother's side. "Mama, what is it?" Hearing the screams of her grandmother brought everyone. Magdalena's grandmother paid no attention to her son, but headed toward the truck, still piled high with their family belongings. She appeared as if she was running from a monster. "This is a *maligno* place. We must all go," she said, waving her hands.

"What are you saying, Mama?" Del asked trying to calm her. "What's the matter with her," he asked his father who had just reached the front door.

Wringing his hands, Del's father shook his head. "There are tiles with the Fascist eagle above the sink, just like during the war. She was forced to work in a big kitchen like this one. Mussolini was feeding his army, and young strong women were needed. This place is too much like the one she worked in She will not stay here, Dominic.

No one could convince Grandma to stay, and within the hour, Magdalena's grandparents were gone, along with Paola, who also believed in the curse, and the entire truck load of furniture, all on their way back to Little Italy.

The men sent to unload the D'Alessandro belongings were sent home. They shook their heads whispering in Italian that the old lady might be right.

Angelina held her father's hand tight. "Daddy, what about our beds?"

"We will buy new ones," he said as he held Angelina close. "Wouldn't you and Magdalena like to pick out brand new bedroom furniture? You each have your own room now."

Magdalena watched as Angelina threw her arms around her father and looked up at him with her large blue eyes. He bent down to Angelina's face, and spoke softly to his ten-year-old. "You are so fair and beautiful, just like your mother." After the shock of the grandparents leaving, no one had anything much to say, but Magdalena asked. "Papa, will grandma and grandpa return to their flat in Little Italy?"

"Yes, they will. I didn't have time to rent it out before we left. So, yes, they'll have their old place to return to, and that's why I let them take all the furniture."

Magdalena offered, "Maybe, I could write them a letter and tell them how we miss them, and we would like them to come back."

With a faraway look Del said, "Yes, that would be nice, but to see them again I think we'll have to visit them in Little Italy." He spoke with a finality that surprised Magdalena.

The morning slowly passed as the balance of the family sat around a large kitchen table, picked at the groceries from the Cozzas and the fruit from the large cellophane basket the realtor had left. Magdalena found a card, signed Jimmy Sciacca. She didn't know why, but decided to keep the card and not mention it to her father. She stood and walked to him putting her hand on his shoulder. "Papa, why don't you find Gino, and explore the grounds. Angelina and I will go upstairs and unpack our suitcases. We haven't even seen the bedrooms yet. Paola said one was huge and had a fireplace. He nodded, and ambled to the front door to tour the beautiful four-acre estate with the cursed kitchen."

*****

In her bathing suit, Magdalena climbed the few steps

out of the pool, reached for her terry rob then took the elevator to the foyer. They had lived in the house for just a few days, but she had already begun her regimen to swim early each morning.

As Magdalena turned to walk up the stairs to her room, she paused at the landing where a window streamed sunshine. Below her she heard her father and Gino talking. It was nice to see a friendship grow between her father and Gino, the stocky little caretaker. Gino was explaining the grounds in detail; the exotic and imported plants, the flowerbeds and mature trees. Her father's interest in the gardens seemed to blossom with the endless varieties of plants that Gino detailed. She could hear Gino's description in his thick Italian accent: "One hundred and thirty-eight roses, forty-two avocado trees," he said, waving his cap toward the grove.

"Come, I show you the koi fish pond. Then we see the cactus and succulent gardens. Like Italy, the soil she is rich, anything will grow here. I can grow you some *verduras* too."

"Fresh vegetables would be nice, but what we really need now is a cook," lamented Del.

"A cook? My sister, she's a cook. Maria works for families all over this - place, long-a time.

"Is she available?"

"Right now."

"She's hired."

Gino shrugged. "We'll see. I tell her to come tomorrow and talk about it. Okay?"

Del was surprised, but nodded, "Okay."

*****

The following day, a freshly scrubbed woman in a plain white blouse, dark skirt and sensible shoes rang the doorbell. Like Gino, she was short and squat, with lively dark eyes. Her hair, with a few strands of grey, had been worked into a neat bun. Her neck held a gold cross, and she clutched a worn leather purse.

Angelina had heard they were to have a cook and she was first at the door to greet Maria. "Can you make peanut butter cookies?"

Maria surprised Angelina, reaching for the ten-year old to take her in her arms. "Of course. I make your papa like me, I make peanut butter cookies just for you."

Maria's effusive manner soon drew from everyone what they liked to eat. She seemed to interview the family, rather than the other way around.

After a tour of the kitchen, wrinkling her nose at a few things, she told Del, "Okay, I take job. I will not live in the house. I have my own little place. But I always arrive early for breakfasts and you get a big dinner out of me," she assured them.

The next day, directly after her arrival, she gave the kitchen a thorough scrubbing, and she settled in. Soon Maria pleased everyone with her Italian specialties and good nature. She took to Angelina with considerable affection, almost like a surrogate mother. Angelina and the cook were getting too close, Magdalena thought. Maria hugged her, baked for her and listened to her ramble on about any subject. *Angelina must miss Mama more than I knew.* I guess Mama always gave Angelina the affection she craved. I had twelve years with Mama; Angelina had only five. We are very different. Angelina is the extrovert and needs lots of affection. That was taken away when Mama died.

After several weeks, Magdalena was concerned about how much time Angelina spent in the kitchen.

"Maria, can we speak?" Magdalena said sitting at the big round kitchen table.

"We can talk, but I have to stand and stir the Bolognaise sauce," waving a wooden spoon at the pot on the stove.

Magdalena cleared her throat. "You seem to be spending a lot of time with Angelina, almost as though you were her mother."

Maria turned away from the stove, one hand on her hip, and eyed the fifteen-year-old. "So, *you* want to be her mother?"

"I didn't say that, I just think you should know that you are *not her mother*, and please do not try to be."

"I should know that I am not Angelina's mother? Is that what you are telling me?"

"Yes, I think that is what I mean." Magdalena said, trying to hold her own in a conversation she was not sure she should have started.

Maria's eyes narrowed. "And your cold ways are going to make her happy?"

Magdalena didn't know how to answer that remark.

"Angelina come to my kitchen to eat, yes. But most of all she come for love. As long as she come to my kitchen, I will give her food and care, unless you want to fire me."

"No, I didn't say that, Maria. I can't fire you."

"Yes, you can. You want me to go, I go right now." Your Papa find somebody else. Then say nothing more. My sauce come out not so good when I get mad."

Magdalena got up and left the kitchen. As she entered the dining room she saw her father stepping out of his office. "What is Maria cooking tonight? It smells wonderful."

"A Bolognaise sauce for pasta."

"Can that woman cook! We are so lucky to have her, Del said, rubbing his hands together."

"Yes, Papa."

Chapter 5

In bed that night, Magdalena reviewed in her mind her conversation with Maria. Maternal attention, frequent hugs and lots of peanut butter cookies probably made Angelina happy. *Maybe one day I could apologize to Maria for criticizing her way with Angelina. Not for a while.*

Soon, Maria made it clear that a proper housekeeper was needed for the large home. Once again, Gino was consulted and he sent a candidate. When Del interviewed the woman, he found she, too, was Italian. Her name was Rosella, and she was married to an older man named Alberto, whose last job had been as a chauffeur. He had been without work for many months after a spell of depression. Del inquired further, and Rosella told him the couple had lost their only child in an auto accident the year before. He couldn't help offering her and her husband the apartment above the garage. The couple wept over his generosity.

With the hiring of three new people, the atmosphere of the house warmed considerably. The absence of Del's parents was no longer felt.

*****

Magdalena saw her father settle into a comfortable work routine. He averaged two trips weekly to the Los

Angeles courts. When he returned with the copies of charges filed by the prosecutors, he would prepare his briefs and do research in his elegant library office. She heard Papa arrange a lot of plea bargains, always seeking a way to stay out of court. Magdalena thought his work had become routine, no longer inspiring. It was only when he walked the grounds in the evening with Gino, chatting in Italian, that he seemed happy.

One night, Magdalena heard the phone ring late in the evening. Her father had a brief conversation with someone and after hanging up, came to her bedroom. "I must go out, Magdalena. I'll tell Alberto to keep the big light at the garage on."

"Is something wrong Papa?"

"No, I'll be back soon," he said shutting her door.

Magdalena opened her door a crack and saw her father rush down the stairs. Papa never rushes, she thought. *I wonder what's happened.*

"Goddamn it, Paola is back," Del grumbled to himself as he drove down the long driveway. "And she's up to her old tricks."

*****

Del was advised to take a seat on a worn bench at the Santa Monica Police Department. This place wasn't like San Francisco where officers called him by his first name, and where he could make a special arrangement for a client.

A stern-faced Sergeant Anderson appeared and addressed him curtly, "Mr. D' Alessandro."

"Good evening Officer," Del said extending his hand which the sergeant chose to ignore.

"Sir, we have a Paola Mancuso in custody. She tells us you are both her lawyer and her brother, is that correct?"

"That's correct, Sergeant."

"This way," the Sargent said, heading down a long hall and directing Del into a private office.

Alone, Del stood looking at framed certificates on the walls and photos of public officials on the desktop. A large photograph of the Governor, Ronald Reagan hung prominently on the wall behind the desk. The name, "Captain Carl Mertz" was stenciled on the glass door. Del had decided to stay standing, when a tall, heavy-set man entered with a burst of energy.

"Hello," the man said, offering Del his hand. "I'm Captain Mertz."

"Dominic D'Alessandro, Captain," Del said, feeling small as he shook Mertz's large hand.

"Take a seat. I don't believe we've met." Del felt an implied question. Who is this Italian from the posh suburb of Holmby Hills?

"No, Captain, we haven't. I'm am relatively new counselor in the area." Del hoped the captain had no idea who Del represented. As Mertz sat reviewing the paperwork before him, Del recognized a seasoned, confident officer.

"We picked up a Paola Mancuso for soliciting on the Santa Monica pier," the Captain said, looking up. "She's been booked and is in a holding cell."

Damn, thought Del, *they photographed and fingerprinted her.* His face burning, Del spoke with sincerity. "I'm sorry to hear that, Captain. I was hoping as her brother and counselor, we might work something out." I hate this groveling, he thought.

"Yeah, well for starters, you can tell her not to solicit Johns in my city. It seems she rented skates, then cruised the Santa Monica pier, hitting up all the unaccompanied men she could find." The Captain displayed a trace of a smile. "Has this happened before, Mr. Del Assan…?

"Just call me Del, Captain. I'll be honest; this has happened before. She's a bit demented… and when she gets away from the family, she sometimes does this sort of thing." Del wiggled his finger beside his head.

Nodding, the Captain set the paperwork aside. "Well, we don't know one another, so little can be worked out, especially since she's been booked."

Del sat quietly waiting and wondering if anything good could come of this.

"These ladies come in all shapes, sizes and colors, if you know what I mean,' the Captain continued. Every man has his own fetish!" The Captain rubbed his jaw avoiding a grin. As he leaned back in his chair, a quick laugh followed. "On roller skates - now I've had a lot of hookers come through this station – but on roller skates?" Del saw him shake his head and suppress another laugh. Del didn't share the Captain's humor. "Captain, as her lawyer and relative, can you put her in my custody until a trial date is set?"

*****

Del drove home in silence; his jaw held firm, his temper barely under control, holding his face in an angry scowl. Paola sat quiet and erect in the back seat, wearing a flowered print dress. With a wide-eyed stare, her short hair held back with a large bobby pin, her roller skates on her lap, she looked childish and empty headed.

When the car stopped, Del locked the doors. Clutching the steering wheel, he swore, first in Italian, then in English. He turned to glare at her. "Look at me, *Paola*," but she avoided his scowl.

"The Captain released you in my custody. I have no friends in these courts like I had in San Francisco, so we have to go before a judge and you could go to jail for six months, with a possible five-thousand-dollar fine. *Comprendere, Paola*?"

"*Si* Papa Del, I *comprendere*. Can I keep the roller skates?

"No," he yelled.

*****

Del rose soon after dawn the next day, wanting to speak to Gino. As he walked the grounds looking for him, the aromas from fruit tree blossoms and the smell of freshly turned earth hung in the air. "There you are," Del said, finding Gino uncoiling a large hose.

"*Buongiorno Signore,*" Gino said, "Is everything okay?"

"Yes, yes, fine. I want to talk to you about my *sorella*, Paola."

Gino looked nervous. He dropped the hose and removed his cap. "She came to see me last night for where to get the bus."

"Really, she was here last night?"

Gino nodded, staring at the ground, twisting his cap, unable to look at Del.

"What is it, Gino?"

Discomfort was written all over Gino's face; his voice was almost inaudible. "She tried to come to my bed, I am sorry to tell you this. And for money," he quickly added, "But I say no."

Del hung his head, feeling the anger and shame that Paola stirred in him. "I didn't know, Gino."

"I know, *Signore* Del, but she is not bad, just a little *ottuso*," he said, rotating his finger near his head.

Del nodded, grieved and sympathetic. "Paola just shows up, I guess, when she has nothing else to do. I was thinking, maybe you could find work for her in the garden?

She's afraid of the kitchen, like my Mother."

Eyes wide, Gino shook his head with fervor.

Del responded quickly. "No, no, of course not, I understand,"

"But *Signore* Del, at the church Sunday I heard that Sister Gabriella wants someone to wash the floors and clean the toilets. And I think they have a little room there where Paola could stay."

"Gino, you never fail us. And I regret that I have not been to church here. I must introduce myself to the *Pastor*."

That evening, Del arranged for Gino to take an envelope of cash to Sister Gabriella for taking in Paola, along with a note saying monthly payments would follow.

*****

With a forlorn expression, Paola sat in the back seat of Del's Corvair. A shopping bag sat next to her with all her possessions; her skates were on her lap. "Where are we going, Papa Del?"

"You are going to live at Saint Michael's. It is close by, and they have a special room for you. But of course, you must do some chores for the nuns. Do you understand me, Paola?" He looked at her sad face in his rearview mirror. "Sister Gabriella is waiting for you. Gino arranged it."

Her chin crumpled as she asked, "Can I come to the big house to see my *nipotes*?"

"Yes, maybe once a month," Del said with a lack of enthusiasm.

He stopped the car and watched as she plodded to the church steps then up to the entrance. She looked small beside the two tall doors. When she turned to look back at him with a look of remorse, he waved her on.

One of the huge doors opened with a moan. Sister Gabriella appeared and, looking at the car nodded to

D'Alessandro. Paola's shopping bag was taken from her and Sister Gabriella said, "Follow me."

Paola crossed herself then walked into the dark entry of the church, following the quick steps of Sister Gabriella.

Chapter 6

One morning, Magdalena noticed on her father's desk two worn volumes that surprised her with new insight into his thinking. She browsed through the first book, smiling. It was an old Roman history from a book-finder service in Los Angeles. Her smile retreated when she opened the second volume. Inside was an incomplete letter to an old associate in San Francisco. It stated that her father had freed himself of medical debt, and now wanted out of this 'demeaning practice' of defending criminals, so he might return to the prosecution side of the law. He couldn't take defense work.

Later that evening when her father returned from LA, she stepped into his office. "Hello, Papa," she said, moving to his chair to kiss his forehead. "Are those the books on Roman history?"

His dark, heavy eyebrows rose. "Yes, last night I read about the giant Mastiffs that went into battle with their masters. They were remarkable canines, loyal and brave. But what about you? I've been so busy working in my office, and coming and going to Los Angeles, I haven't had a report on your swimming," he said pushing the books aside, and changing the subject.

Magdalena had hoped that her father would share his thoughts of giving up this lifestyle, but he hadn't. So, she tucked the secret away as he had.

"Oh, I love swimming. It makes me feel alive. I know my leg will always be a little short, but don't worry Papa. It is wonderful to live here where I can always swim. I get up early and go straight to the pool, in our own house. Who can do that? And, Papa, I didn't tell you what I found in an old cabinet downstairs." She waited for her father to place the two history volumes on shelves behind him.

"And what is that Magdalena?" He said, obviously pleased the topic had changed.

"I found boxes of records, all classical music, and a record player. It reminds me of when you and Mama used to listen to classical music." Her father's stare into the distance saddened her. He didn't become maudlin after her mama's name was mentioned anymore, but a long silence would often follow. She waited for his response.

"What kind of records, Magdalena?"

"Whoever the person they belonged to must have loved Rachmaninoff."

Her father nodded, "A Russian pianist, a great composer. I don't know him well but I think he may have written an opera or two. He died not long ago. You should take a class in classical music when you start UCLA. Now I have to get to work."

I wonder when Papa thinks we could move away from this beautiful place? And yet he talks about me attending UCLA. I must always tell him how much I love it here.

*****

The next morning when passing Del's office, Magdalena overheard a phone call. Her father was agreeing to a meeting with a man named, Jimmy Sciacca. That was the name on the card she kept from the fruit basket when they moved in.

Del hung up the phone. "Magdalena," he called.

"Yes, Papa," she said stepping into his office.

"I will leave tomorrow morning and be gone overnight," he said, handing her the number of the Bel Air Hotel. "The hotel is less than a mile down Stone Canyon, but I have evening and morning meetings there so I will spend the night."

"Yes Papa," she said, wide-eyed, realizing that they had never been away from one another overnight. She felt instant concern, but quickly reined in her fearful thoughts.

"You're comfortable being alone for one night, now that Albert and Rosella are living above the garage, aren't you, Magdalena?"

"Yes Papa," she said, realizing how silly it would be to be afraid."

"I will tell Gino to leave the big flood light on," her father said.

Magdalena nodded, trying to remove the veil of concern she knew showed on her face.

When late morning arrived, she waved goodbye to her father without concern. A chauffeur-driven limousine had been sent for him. *Papa looked nice in his blue suit with the fine stripes,* she thought.

*****

The family's first summer had passed in their new house, and it was time to register for school. Magdalena didn't want to burden Papa with this task, and she wanted to get both herself and Angelina well established in school quickly.

After Papa left, Magdalena searched the yellow pages of the telephone directory for the location of the Santa Monica Library. She had questions that could be answered there. Her aim was to take care of all the family business, just as Mama would have.

Magdalena was relieved that she and Angelina could both go to the same school. When she asked Gino to drive her into Santa Monica in his small pick-up truck, he agreed enthusiastically.

On the way to the library, Gino spoke loudly over his truck's noisy engine. "Your papa tells me to leave the big light on all night, *Signorina*, and I will walk around the house when it is dark," he assured her as he pulled to a stop.

"Thank you, Gino. Magdalena didn't want to talk about her father being away, but nevertheless, she found Gino's words comforting.

Once inside the library, she arranged for a card in order to check out books. While there, she discovered that she could look up people. She used the archives of the Los Angeles Times microfiche articles about Jimmy Sciacca, also known as Jimmy Boxer and Dominic Borelli. She read his California career had begun badly when he botched an attempt at killing a major mobster. Now, he headed a thriving crime syndicate in Los Angeles and Orange Counties with an emphasis on loan sharking. She thought of taking notes, but knew she never wanted them found. Magdalena could memorize things easily and decided to do this with these facts about the 'Mafia.' She felt a strong curiosity about secret matters like this.

On a local map, Magdalena located the Catholic school that she and Angelina would attend. She asked the librarian for a bus schedule. The woman offered to help her but Magdalena declined. "I can figure out the bus routes," she said, wanting her home address kept secret.

Magdalena saw the librarian notice her limp when she handed the woman back the schedule and thanked her. The woman paused, then added, "What lovely black hair you have!"

"I appreciate the bus schedules," Magdalena said, embarrassed by the personal compliment. It wasn't the first time a compliment was paid to her after someone noticed her limp.

On the way home, she asked Gino to drive her by Saint Mary's Academy. The white building had been layered into the foothills of the Santa Monica Mountains like a grand Mediterranean monastery. She walked up a long causeway of stairs to the entrance which was surrounded by green lawns, and in the distance, olive trees. After pulling open a heavy wooden door leading to a dark foyer, she found the information desk, where she introduced herself and was given applications for the coming school year. The grammar school and high school shared a campus making it possible for Magdalena to register herself in tenth grade and Angelina in fourth. *Mama would have wanted me to watch over my sister*. Mama once said, *Angelina could be a rebel.*

*****

That night, her father called her from the hotel, and they had a brief conversation. She mentioned that he needed to sign the paperwork on his desk to enroll her and Angelina in St. Mary's Academy. He was pleased she had taken it upon herself to handle this. "Have a good night, and a fine swim in the morning, *Pescolina*. And where is my *Bionda,* Angelina?"

Magdalena brought her sister to the phone then went to her bedroom.

Much later, when she heard her sister come upstairs to bed. Magdalena turned off her light. Sleep didn't come for some time, as one thought kept returning to her. *I wish we had a pair of Mastiffs for our family protection. And it would make Papa so happy.*

Chapter 7

Magdalena had fallen into a deep sleep when repeated chimes of their doorbell woke her. She put on her robe, descended the stairs, and opened the front door. She turned on the outdoor light to peer through the attached entrance, enclosed in glass and wrought iron. There stood an unfamiliar man.

"Hi, I have an important message from Eddy Cavallaro. You want to let me in, *Signorina*?" Said a sweet-talking voice. Magdalena looked through the glass enclosure at a grinning face even a child would recognize as false. His voice came across as artificial with an evil tone, too. She felt somewhat consoled by the safety of the wrought iron enclosure but at the same time frightened and leery. *No one should be at our door this late,* she thought.

"Who are you?" asked Magdalena pushing back strands of her hair. But when he answered, his cunning voice continued to riddle her with fear.

"Just open the gate, *Signorina*, I have a special file for your father, from Eddy." He held one hand behind him.

Magdalena shook her head and stepped back. "I don't know you. Come tomorrow when my father's home." Quivering, she retreated, immediately regretting she had revealed her father wasn't at home.

Overlooking the garage court stood the second-story apartment of Rosella and Alberto.

"Who is there? What do you want?" Called Alberto, leaning out his upstairs window.

"Go back to bed, old man," countered the intruder as he worked to pry open the gate.

Magdalena watched in horror as the man stubbornly levered the iron-gate open. She backed into the house to shut the front door. Behind her, she heard Angelina calling to her from the top of the stairs. "Go back to your room, Angelina, and lock yourself in," Magdalena said, fumbling to shut the massive wooden door.

"What is it?" Angelina cried.

Magdalena turned toward her sister. and yelled. "Do as I say, Angelina, and now!"

In those few seconds of distraction, the man had ruptured the outside paddle lock and flung open the iron-gate. At the same time, Magdalena got front door closed, but couldn't secure the dead bolt. She could feel the man's heavy weight pushing at the mahogany door that she desperately tried to hold closed. For a moment, she thought she was gaining against his strength. Her hands shook. Then the man lunged opening the door. When Magdalena saw his foot wedged across the threshold, she turned and ran for the stairs.

*****

Del had arrived at the hotel in plenty of time to unpack his suitcase in the bungalow and go wander the grounds of this storybook hotel, a hideaway for well-healed Holmby Hill residences and Hollywood people. After his walk around the lake, where swans paddled about, he marveled at the lush landscape then located the bar for his dinner meeting. A headwaiter led him through the paneled cocktail lounge and to a tufted red leather booth where a man awaited his arrival. The scent of citrus cologne surrounded the man who wore a dark grey suit, a black silk shirt and white tie.

Jimmy Sciacca with his pocked face and thick eyebrows looked the part of a mobster. He had joined the gambling syndicate of Mickey Cohen in 1940, but soon defected to Jack Dragna's L.A. crime family. In 1947, he became a made-man under Dragna. Working in loan sharking, he was promoted to *caporegime* in Orange County.

"Your guest has arrived, Mr. Sciacca," said the waiter outfitted in an impeccable tuxedo.

"Thanks," Sciacca said indicating a place near him in the booth. "Del, have a seat. It's good of you to come."

Sciacca's voice was deep with a calm demeanor. "How about a cocktail?" He signaled the waiter over.

"I'm not drinking," Del said in a rougher voice than he had intended.

"They've got some great reds here." Sciacca said, encouraging Del to loosen up.

Del nodded, "I'll try a red," he said, deciding to look interested.

"Bring us a bottle of that Barolo that I had last night," Sciacca said. The waiter bowed and disappeared.

Although Del knew little of wine, he reasoned that a warm red might be a good antidote to the bad taste in his mouth this meeting was already giving him.

"This is a great restaurant. Best steaks, best wine and Hollywood people love it here," Sciacca said with the confidence of a man who ate and drank the best of everything.

Del nodded finding himself unable to make small talk.

He knew he had to stifle old hatreds boiled up inside him as Del sat across from Sciacca. He had prosecuted these types in the federal courts after studying his way into law school, and out of the slums of Little Italy. These were strong memories he had to get past. But, he also had to remember that Sciacca allowed for the villa his family lived in.

"The house we settled in is very nice for my family, Mr. Sciacca." Del said speaking with all the politeness he could muster.

"Yeah, I hear it's a palace. Even got an indoor pool. I also hear your oldest kid has to swim to help her polio. That's tough." Sciacca said lighting up a small cigar.

"She swims every day." Del didn't like that Sciacca knew things about his daughters.

"The family has to be taken care of," Sciacca said, his words sounding sincere. "But I want to talk business. You're doing good for us as our in-house counsel. You get a lot of counts struck from complaints, you settle a lot of stuff out of court. We like that," Sciacca said with the seriousness of a judge. "Porterhouse steaks okay with you?" He said, waving the waiter back to their table.

Del nodded, wondering why these guys all wore those goddam pinky rings mounted with a big diamond.

When the steak arrived, it was clear this was no ordinary meal. It was a feast, with a piece of meat that covered the plank it was served on. Side dishes filled the table. The over-sized, serrated knife that came with the meat looked like an apt metaphor for the meeting to Del.

With little conversation passing between them, the men carved their tender steaks and ate in silence. Finally, they sat back, stuffed with the rich food, and Sciacca broached a subject that had been left to the end of the meal. "You've been with us less than a year. You're good "D'Alessandro.

I told you Cavallaro tried to weasel into our L.A. port business, and I wanted you to go after him. And you did it fast. I don't know how you did it. I don't want to know how you did it."

What Del could not tell Sciacca was that he turned Cavallaro over to an old FBI friend. Del hadn't felt so good in months. Cavallaro had been promptly tried in federal court, convicted and about to serve his time in Federal prison as they spoke.

Sciacca put a hand on Del's arm. "But I've got to tell you something about Cavallaro. He's a vengeful man. If he tries to send a message to you, in any way, you call me."

Unnerved by Sciacca's comment, Del had trouble controlling his words. *Christ. Why would he contact me?*

"I'm just saying if. But don't worry it's probably no big deal," countered Sciacca as he waved for the waiter.

It sounds like you've given me good reason to worry! Del's thoughts returned to his home and daughters, alone with little Gino, and a measly floodlight. *Jesus what a life I've bought into.*

"Listen Del, I gotta go. You'll be okay," Sciacca said punching out his cigar, and tossing a hundred-dollar bill on the check. "I'll have the Cozza brothers hang around for a few weeks for protection." Then pushing a business card across the table, he added. "I want you to do something before you go back home."

"What's that?" Del said, absently, thinking about the limited measures of security he had employed at home. "Get some suits made by my tailor in LA. You dress like a law clerk, not a counselor."

And you dress like a pimp.

The waiter approached their table. "Yeah, what is it?" asked Sciacca.

"There is an urgent message, sir, for Mr. D'Alessandro to call St John's hospital in Santa Monica."

Chapter 8

"Bring me a phone and the number," demanded Sciacca. In seconds the waiter returned with a telephone, plugged it into the table jack, handed Del the number on a 3 by 5 card, and retreated. Sciacca took the card from Del and dialed the number. When someone answered, he said, "You have a new patient there name of D'Alessandro…? Yeah, Magdalena Del'Alessandro., this is her father speaking. Thanks."

Del was angered by Sciacca's dominating the situation but had no time to object before Sciacca handed him the phone.

With the receiver held tightly to his head, Del said, "My daughter, what has happened? Assaulted how? I mean how badly?" Del turned gray just listening to a summary of Magdalena's injuries. He tightened one hand into a fist, and frowned at Sciacca. "And my daughter, Angelina, was she injured?" Del was relieved to hear Angelina was not injured? Who is this man you say was brought in with my daughter?... And, no I don't know either."

"Can't I speak with Magdalena?" Del anxiously asked? "No? Why not? Oh, sedated, of course. How long?"

"Maybe when she is awake. You could talk to her then," the doctor said.

"Okay, I will be there as soon as possible."

Del held the receiver in his hand long after the line went dead, intently mulling the final words about Magdalena's condition. He glared at Sciacca, and with mounting anger, spoke through his teeth. "Magdalena has a broken arm and is badly beaten. She was brought in with another man who is in intensive care." They don't have a name, but I think its Gino, my gardener."

Sciacca remained silent while Del struggled for self-control. "It is bad that your family has been attacked. I'll handle this."

The large meal Del had consumed suddenly felt like acid roiling in his gut. His body was on fire, there was a foul taste in his mouth, and his heart raced. "The police have already been to the house to investigate. I must leave immediately."

"I'll take it from here," Sciacca said. "You go to your daughter. I'll have my limo waiting out front for you." Sciacca said." He nodded, and left.

*****

The wind was cool for an early autumn day in Los Angeles, as the limousine drove Dominic D'Alessandro toward the Santa Monica hospital. Leaves swirled in the streets. The smooth sound of the Eagles singing Hotel California did nothing to ease Del's anxiety. He knew his blood pressure, if measured today would be off the charts. Seated in the spacious back of the car, he admonished himself for allowing his life to arrive at this place.

He asked, knocking on the glass that separated him from the driver, "How long to get to the hospital?" The man lowered the partition electronically. "There's a device back there that you can use to talk to me, Mr. D'Alessandro.

"I don't give a fuck about the device, how much longer,

I asked."

"About a half an hour, sir."

Del's mind was reeling with concern over Magdalena's beating. The doctor had said she had facial wounds as well as a broken arm. Sixteen-year-old Magdalena battered by whom? But, of course, after his conversation with Sciacca he knew it was retribution for putting away that goddam Eddie Cavallaro. *And Angelina, oh my God, she must be frightened to death.*

When the car phone next to Del rang, he jerked like a scared kid. "Hello,' he yelled into the receiver.

"Hello, Mr. D'Alessandro," said a calm voice. "This is Lenny Sheldon, Mr. Sciacca's accountant." A silence ensued.

"Yes," Del finally answered with a limited measure of calm.

"I have been instructed to tell you that all hospital expenses will be taken care of for your daughter, as well as your associate who defended her. Mr. Sciacca offers his condolences for what has happened."

"How the hell do you know that the man in intensive care defended my daughter?" Del shouted into the phone.

"Mr. Sciacca has determined that, Mr. D'Alessandro, and wants you to know that the man responsible will not be battering you or your family ever again."

There was a long pause. "What is the man's name who defended my daughter?" asked Del, visualizing little Gino in intensive care.

"His name is Alberto, sir."

With another pause, and sigh of relief, Del dispelled his image of a battered Gino.

"Mr. D'Alessandro, are you still there?" asked the accountant.

"Yes, yes," Del said, slowly grasping that the housekeeper's husband Alberto lay in the hospital, hanging onto his life.

"Mr. Sciacca informed me that I am to help you in any way I can," said the accountant.

Del gained some control. As a lawyer, he decided exactly what help he wanted. "Oh, did he?" Del paused to control his furor over the attack on Magdalena, and Alberto. "Well, this is what I want. No more envelopes of cash from his soldiers, or whatever you call your henchmen. For Chris sake, this is the seventies. I want a corporate account, set up in my name and my $25,000 monthly salary deposited in it with proper tax withholding. I want a car and resident chauffeur, as well as helicopter service when I need it for urgent court appearances. Do you have all of that? And what did you say your name was?"

"Lenny Sheldon, Mr. D'Alessandro.

"Do you foresee any problems with what I've outlined, Lenny?"

"No sir, I do not."

Chapter 9

The police who had escorted the ambulance to the hospital the prior evening told the admitting doctor that both victims had suffered brutal attacks by a man wielding a tire iron. They thought the man was near death. The police had arrived at the estate too late to apprehend the attacker but said they would pursue the case with serious interest.

The ambulance had taken Magdalena and Alberto to the Santa Monica hospital. Alberto's wife Rosella rode in the ambulance hysterically explaining to the paramedics how her husband tried to defend Magdalena.

*****

The next morning, Magdalena awoke in her hospital bed. When she tried to smile at the nurse who entered her room, a network of pain migrated across her face. One partly closed eye, now the size of an egg, shone bright red. Her lower lip looked like a piece of frayed rope. With a bandage on her head and her arm in a sling, she resembled a casualty from a serious automobile accident.

Another nurse arrived at Magdalena's hospital room maneuvering through the door with a huge bouquet. "My, I don't think I have ever seen so many pink roses in one vase. I counted three dozen. You must be loved very much, young lady," the nurse said, looking at Magdalena's mutilated face.

Magdalena peeked through her one good eye. She shuddered briefly when a flash of her assailant returned. Although the memory of his face was elusive, she remembered he'd said he was sent by Eddy Cavallaro.

"You were brought in last night, Magdalena," the nurse said, reading her chart. "Your wounds have all been stitched and you just need rest, dear," added the nurse, avoiding the subject of her brutal attack. "Your father has been notified, and I believe is on his way to see you."

*****

The sun setting over the Pacific Ocean colored the Santa Monica Mountains dark purple. Orange and red colors painted the sky like a giant watercolor.

At sunset, Del stepped from the limo and rushed to the hospital entrance. Apprehensive, he pushed open the heavy door. In the recent past, he had spent many hours in hospitals during his wife's death from breast cancer. The regular visits he'd made to her bedside during that dismal period eroded his spirit so that hospitals nearly caused him to panic. And trips he made with Magdalena to the polio clinic only further tapped his emotional strength. Both experiences diminished his capacity to be among suffering people. Trying to show control, he inquired at the reception desk in a strong voice. But when young Angelina came running, calling out to him, Del faltered physically and emotionally. "Thank God, thank God, it wasn't you Angelina," he said as he held her close.

"Daddy, Daddy Magdalena looks terrible," Angelina said. "Some horrible man beat her up, and Alberto, too."

Del's felt some relief as he held on tight to Angelina. Together they walked to Rosella, who was seated quietly in a waiting area. "This is terrible; I am so sorry," Del said, looking down into her tear-stained face and taking her hand in his. Her face was consumed with fear, and Del surmised that it wasn't clear if Alberto would live or die. He turned to Angelina and took some time to quiet her with hugs and kisses. Del acknowledged Gino and his sister, Maria, with a resigned nod. He didn't want to ask, but reasoned that his household staff and Angelina had been at the hospital all night, waiting on news about Alberto's survival. A nurse appeared and motioned Del to follow her to Magdalena's room.

*****

When her father came into Magdalena's blurry view, she looked at his contorted face and knew he was a victim in this attack almost as much as she. His expression grew dark as he observed her bandages and lacerations.

"I have done the wrong thing working for these people. Your mother would be sick if she was alive." Magdalena, still feeling the effects of sedation, managed to slur, "Thank you for the roses." After that she dropped off to sleep.

The nurse entered. "Your daughter needs rest now, Mr. D'Alessandro. You can stay here while she sleeps, or you may wait in the reception room. I'll can call you when she awakens."

When Del stood to leave Magdalena's room, he reached for the small envelope on the rose bouquet. 'Condolences from Jimmy Sciacca,' the card read. Del's tore the card into small pieces before tossing it into the wastebasket next to Magdalena's bed.

*****

Sciacca had been assigned to secure D'Alessandro as counselor for the Organization, and had been with them less than a year. Now there was a strong possibility that D'Alessandro would walk away from his position after the attack on his daughter. It was necessary that Sciacca moved fast to try and stop that. He started by taking care of the hospital costs, acceding to D'Alessandro's demands and sending flowers to Magdalena. Whatever it took to maintain D'Alessandro as the Family's lawyer, Sciacca would do.

Once jailed, Cavallaro had moved fast for his revenge. Sciacca hadn't moved at the same speed, now Sciacca had to clean up the mess. Elimination plans for Cavallaro, once he was incarcerated, were to take place with inside connections. No one who crossed the Family lived long, in or out of prison.

After Sciacca got off the phone with his accountant, the Cozza brothers were notified. Sciacca growled into the receiver, "I want the son-of-a-bitch that went after Magdalena hit, now!"

Joey and Vinnie were surprised to learn of the brutal attack on Magdalena. Sciacca's vehement order and his compassion for Magdalena caught them off guard. The brothers had never seen their boss so outraged. The hired thug was easy to find, and the Cozza's did as instructed. They knew the guy liked poker. That night Joey and Vinnie waited in an alley outside a door where a high-stakes poker game was played. When the game ended, the thug walked out into the alley, each brother took an arm and walked him down to the dark end. Vinnie, quickly slit his throat at the jugular. Joey lifted him, upside down into an empty trash can.

*****

With no family, Sciacca was easily developing a strong affection for Magdalena. He had reasoned that it was God's will that the old man Alberto had saved her life, and that enough sorrow had come to her for one lifetime.

*****

That evening at the hospital, after Magdalena said good night to her father, she received a brief note from Sciacca. It was hand delivered by Vinnie and Joey. The brothers politely added their sympathies and respects, then promptly left.

Sciacca's note read: *Signoria Magdalena, my condolences to you for what happened. This problem has been taken care of, and will never happen again. In the future, I want you to think of me as your friend and protector. Call me if you ever need anything, Jimmy Sciacca.*

Magdalena lay pensive as she held the message in her lap, and memorized Sciacca's telephone number. With difficulty, she tore up the note and deposited it in the same wastebasket where her father had disposed of Sciacca's sympathy card.

Outside the hospital, getting into their car, Vinnie turned to Joey. "Jesus, what a creep that Cavallaro was to hire a hit on such a young one."

Joey lit a cigarette. "Yeah, and how about the old man who saved her? His balls must be the size eggplants."

Vinnie smirked, "Yeah, another tough Guinea."

*****

The doctor entered the waiting room of the hospital, walked to Del and turned to Rosella, who immediately stood. "Your husband's condition has stabilized, and we will move him from intensive care to a private room in a few days. I must tell you, he is a very strong man to have come through this appalling beating. It will be a long recovery for him, Ma'am." Rosella dropped into her chair sobbing, this time with relief.

The doctor continued, "I understand you are the housekeeper at the D'Alessandro's home?" He said putting a hand on her shoulder.

Rosella nodded.

"Your husband is a very brave man and may well have saved the life of your employer's daughter. It appears he intervened and clearly took the brunt of a terrible beating."

Rosella continued to nod through her tears. She had reverted to speaking in Italian. "*Si, si,*" she said.

Del could only stand and listen. Angelina's arms were around her father, fear in her eyes. "Will Magdalena die?" she asked the doctor.

"No, no young lady, your sister will recover fully," he said, smiling down at the frightened ten-year-old.

Chapter 10

Magdalena was able to leave the hospital in ten days, but Alberto had to recuperate there for several weeks. Magdalena was relieved that the school semester had just ended and the entire summer could be a time to recuperate at the villa. She saw that her father seemed greatly relieved by her recovery, but she also saw a decline in his enthusiasm for everything. A slumped posture, noticeable graying, and a perennial frown marked him. She learned he had begun taking medication for high blood pressure, and wondered what she could do to help him.

By the time school began, the cast had been removed from her arm and her facial lacerations had healed. As months passed, the trauma Magdalena and Alberto had suffered began to fade.

*****

School dominated Magdalena and Angelina's conversations on the now-familiar bus ride to Saint Mary's Academy. They had attended their private school for two years, now, and during that time, Magdalena tried to help her younger sister with her studies, but her effort drew little success.

After a long silence on the bus one morning, Angelina turned and looked intently into her sister's face. "Does

Daddy really know who attacked you and Alberto, Magdalena?"

"I'm not sure anybody knows, Angelina," Magdalena lied. "The police came up with no suspects. It's been two years now We'll probably will never know."

As her father became less and less communicative, Magdalena developed the habit of looking through his case file records. One evening, she found a file marked, 'Cavallaro.' She shivered when she read the name. She remembered the night she was assaulted, the man at the door said Cavallaro had sent him. She never got any information about who was responsible for the attack, but likely this was the man. At home, it was never discussed.

"It must have something to do with the Mafia," Angelina said. Shocked, Magdalena sat up straight in her seat. "What makes you use that word?"

"Because I heard Mrs. Manners at the last horse show say that's who Daddy works for."

"Really, and who is Mrs. Manners?" Magdalena asked, trying not to show dislike for someone who had such private information about her father.

"She's in charge of all the local horse shows. She knows everything."

"Oh, does she?" Magdalena said, stalling for time to come up with an answer, and not wanting to discuss the Family her father worked for. Magdalena shifted to Angelina's favorite topic. "Speaking of horse shows, I saw that you won a blue ribbon at the last one. You really like riding, don't you, Angelina?"

"I think I like it as much as you like studying. And don't call me Angelina anymore. I am 'Angie' at the barn."

Without reacting to that, Magdalena continued to query her sister. "Tell me about the people at the barn."

"It's my favorite place. I take lessons on this super horse that was brought here from the east coast. No one can ride him except my trainer and me. He says Daddy should buy him for me."

"Really?" What is the cost of the horse?" asked Magdalena.

"Ten thousand dollars," answered Angelina casually.

*****

Magdalena and Alberto were strolling in the garden one morning. He was still walking with a cane, but doing well after returning home from his long stay at a convalescent hospital. Magdalena still found it hard to look at the man who had suffered such brutality while defending her.

She heard a car in the garage court. Uneasy about unknown visitors, Alberto disappeared behind a large bougainvillea. Relieved to see the familiar brothers, Magdalena walked toward the court and told Alberto, "It's the Cozza brothers."

Alberto nodded and walked off.

"Good day, *Signorina*," Joey said.

"Hello," Magdalena responded politely but without emotion. "If you have something for my father please leave it with me; he is away."

"The envelope is for you, *Signorina*. It is from Mr. Sciacca, and he would like an answer, if it is not too much trouble," said Joseph, the older brother.

Magdalena reached for the envelope with a frown. "I will read it and be right back." She walked to the house in her fastest half-step embarrassed to reveal her limp.

"No rush, *Signorina*," Joey said. "We can wait."

She stepped into her father's office for privacy. The note had but two sentences: "*Dear Signorina, I hear you are back to normal. I don't want you to forget to ask me for a favor for you or the family, J. Sciacca."* Magdalena was comfortable with this clandestine means of communication, and it didn't take her long to decide on her favor from Jimmy Sciacca. She quickly wrote her request on the same card, resealed the envelope and returned it to the Cozza brothers with thanks.

*****

Magdalena entered her father's office, went to his side and kissed him on his forehead. "Now, Papa, on Sunday we are all going to a horse show," she said.

"Are we?"

"Yes. Did you know Angelina has been taking equestrian lessons for two years? There is a local show where she will compete, and I told her we would come."

"I am proud that you have arranged these lessons for your sister. Does Angelina like this sport?" her father asked.

"Not only does she like it, but her trainer says she is a talented rider. Have you seen all the blue ribbons in Angelina's room, Papa?"

His face brightened, and he nodded. "That doesn't surprise me; there is the champion in her even if the nuns can't get her to study. Maybe this is where her aptitude lies," he added with some resignation.

Magdalena liked seeing her father's face smile. There had been too few for some time, and they were mostly for Angelina. "I must tell you, Papa, that Angelina is riding a horse Sunday that she wins on often. She and her trainer want you to buy him for her."

"Really? And what does this horse cost?" Del asked.

When Magdalena revealed the price of the animal, she was surprised how quickly her father embraced the idea of buying it for Angelina. *This must mean Papa has decided to live the lifestyle the Family is giving us. Or maybe he loves Angelina a little more.* Either way, she felt more confident that they would stay in this beautiful house, in this wonderful place, forever.

*****

Gino ran ahead of a large white van, guiding it up the long drive to the car court, waving his cap he called, "*Signore, Signore…!*" Magdalena looked out her bedroom window.

Saturday mornings found Magdalena studying and Angelina at the barn, riding. Magdalena quickly descended the staircase and saw her father rushing to the front door from his downstairs office. Outside, Magdalena watched a man step from the van, open the back doors and set two crates on the ground. "What is this?" Del asked. He could get no information from Gino, who was far too excited to be intelligible.

Magdalena came up behind her father and smiled at the canine carriers sitting on the ground. She watched her father's mood soften when he looked inside the crates and saw a pair of twelve-week old mastiff puppies. "This is the D'Alessandro residence, isn't it?" the driver asked.

"Well, yes but who sent these dogs?" Del asked.

"Sir, I was told to deliver them to Dominic D'Alessandro, and to explain how to care for them. They were bred at Mar Vista Kennels," the man said with pride.

"But who are they from?" asked her father.

By now, Rosella and Alberto had come down the stairs from their garage apartment. Maria was wiping her hands on her apron as she arrived from the kitchen to see about the excitement.

"Magdalena stepped forward, "Papa, this is a birthday gift from all of us to you." She turned to peer directly into everyone's face, nodding her head. In wonderment, the group looked at one another but said nothing to the contrary.

The two faun-colored dogs were released from their carriers to wobble around the garage court. Walking like yearlings and sniffing the ground of their new home with their black square mussels, their wagging tails put a smile on all who watched them.

That afternoon, Gino was sent to buy doghouses, food and leashes. That evening, Magdalena's father and Gino took the two dogs on a walk around the grounds. They returned calling the gangly puppies, Romulus and Remus.

Maybe Papa will be happier now with his prized pets, maybe his blood pressure will even come down. She hoped that with the company of the dogs he admired and read so much about in Roman histories, he would have another good reason not to leave this way of life. *I'm making top grades and Angelina is winning at all the horse shows. We have a loyal household staff. Oh, I hope we live here forever...*

Magdalena said a long prayer that night for this to come true. She also wrote a thank you to Jimmy Sciacca for filling her request by sending the dogs. She secreted the note in her dictionary that sat high on her bookshelf and would give it to the Cozza brothers when she next saw them.

Chapter 11

In Magdalena's senior year at Saint Mary's, she led her classmates in most subjects, and the nuns regularly showered her with praise. She had always tried to keep a low profile at school, and found it embarrassing to be singled out for academic excellence. Her subdued, circumspect manner allowed her to solve both family and school problems with emotional composure. She strained only to keep it a secret that her father lawyered for the Organization and to keep the lid on Angelina's volatile behavior.

She couldn't wait to enter college, where she would meld into the numbers without the scrutiny that was so pervasive at Saint Mary's.

She did a good job of juggling her objectives, but a new personal issue perplexed her, angered her, and ultimately caused her to retaliate. At school one day, a tiny roll of paper almost insignificant enough to toss into a wastebasket appeared on her desk. Curiosity led her to unroll it. Two words were neatly printed in ballpoint pen **Gimpy Wop**. Magdalena recalled reading about the racial slur that had become an acronym meaning, 'without papers.' It had applied to Italian immigrants a century earlier. And she certainly knew what gimpy meant. It was an unspeakably rude way of referring to her limp. A pain wrenched her gut after reading the words. She raised her hand to be excused to go to the restroom.

Magdalena splashed cold water on her hot, red face that burned with fury. She forced herself to stop gagging, looked at herself in the mirror and said, "I will know my enemy." With control and determination, she stepped outside to the restroom and positioned herself where she could watch her classmates exit, one by one from class. Intently, she connected with the face of each of the twelve students leaving her small English class. By the time she had viewed the last student in her class, she knew who had written the note, and with calculated interest began to plan her revenge.

*****

The two sisters were on their bus ride home when Magdalena decided to broach the subject of the note she had received in class that day. Not wanting to reveal her hatred for her classmate and the revenge she planned. Magdalena spoke quietly. "Angie, there is a girl named Tracy Manners in my English class. Is she related to the woman who runs the local horseshows you've mentioned?"

"Yep, and she's a bitch, just like her mother," Angie blurted.

Now, in her early teens, Angie had begun to lace much of what she said with swear words and had acquired a collection of epithets. Magdalena didn't often comment about this because she knew Angelina used these words largely for shock value. Besides, Angie didn't use profanity at home, nor did she stay too long with her fads. Horses were the constant in her life. "Why do you say that, Angie?"

"Well, for openers, she hates me because I ride better than she can, even though she's *your* age. Then there's her mother, who rips into her when she doesn't get a ribbon, which is like all the time! Why do you ask? Does Tracy hate you, too?"

Angie had a way of getting to the quick of a subject. "No, I just connected the Manner's name that you have mentioned with the horseshow organizer."

"You're lying. She hates you too," Angie blurted again.

Magdalena relented. "Okay, suppose she does. What do you know about Tracy?"

"She's kind of slutty," Angie casually replied.

"Really? What do you mean by that?"

"Well, for one thing, she goes into empty stalls with trainers and hangs out with the doors closed. And when they split, you can tell they've been fooling around."

"How can you be so sure about that?" Magdalena asked.

"Well she never goes into a stall with a trainer who likes guys."

Magdalena looked puzzled, "And most of the trainers like guys?"

"Ah, yeah, Em," as she had begun referring to her sister. "Didn't you know that?"

When the bus stopped and the doors opened Romulus and Remus came romping toward them. "Hi guys," Angie called then sat down on the driveway to let them slobber all over her. "I love these dogs," she said.

Magdalena waited while Angie had her time with the dogs. As the two walked up the long drive to the house, Angie's face bore a devilish smile.

"Em, Can I borrow that Polaroid camera Daddy got you for Christmas?"

Magdalena saw the expression of an opportunist on Angie's face, and knew her sister was looking for a little revenge of her own. Not asking any further questions,

Magdalena agreed to lend her camera to Angie.

*****

Magdalena's daily swim in the villa's downstairs pool brought her continued comfort. This warm environment had become her exercise and her solace. Lap after lap, she planned her day or worked out a problem. In the four years that they had lived in their stately home, she had never missed her morning swim. That discipline had availed her physical and emotional endurance, and afterwards, a great sense of calm.

Yet recently, a persistent lower back pain began to plague her. It never left, and throughout her day, she winced with pain when she walked.

Never wanting to burden her father with a problem, Magdalena turned to Sciacca, by mail, for an answer. Responding like the friend he had declared himself, Sciacca's return note said he had made calls and arranged an immediate doctor appointment for her. He added that if the doctor could not help her, he would also arrange for a specialist.

Gino drove her to the Santa Monica hospital where she saw the doctor who cared for her four years earlier. Magdalena hoped that a specialist wouldn't be needed, and with apprehension, kept her appointment.

*****

"Hello Magdalena. My, you have grown into an attractive young woman since I last saw you. You're nearly eighteen, and about to go to college."

"Yes, I have applied to UCLA and Berkeley," she said softly. Looking at his chart, the doctor seemed confused. "Who is this Mr. Sciacca that called, insisting that he speak to me about you?"

"He is sort of my uncle. My father is away a lot, and

my mother past away several years ago." Magdalena answered.

"I see. He seemed most concerned about your back pain." He walked around Magdalena's chair to get to his desk noticing her well-formed breasts along the way.

Magdalena nodded, "It has become constant. I was hoping you could give me something for it," she said, not wanting to linger on the subject of Sciacca.

After a thorough examination, Magdalena dressed, and the nurse directed her to the doctor's office. She settled in a chair across from the doctor's desk and hoped he would prescribe her a pain medicine.

"Your uncle, Mr. Sciacca, was quite adamant about me sending you to a specialist but I believe a specialist would tell you the same thing I'm about to. You suffered polio in pubescence, is that correct?"

Magdalena nodded.

"And it left you with one leg a bit shorter."

Magdalena nodded again.

"I am quite surprised that you haven't corrected your footwear to accommodate this condition. When you do, I think you'll find the back pain will disappear. He took one more glance at her breasts. Your uneven step is causing pressure on your lower back. A simple adjustment to your shoes should take care of the problem."

Magdalena had refused to address her limp, not wanting to make it a problem or bring unnecessary attention to her. She had grown skilled at walking, smoothly making her faulty step often appear normal. "So, a special shoe that raises me up on that side?" she said.

"It's that simple, my dear." Then, a last glance.

"Thank you, doctor." *Oh, I hope it is that simple.*

*****

On the ride home in Gino's truck, Magdalena explained her need to find someone to alter her shoes. Gino's chest grew as he announced, "Ah, Gino knows the man, my cousin. He has the best shoe shop in Santa Monica."

Little Gino always knew how to help the family. *What would we do without him?* "Can you take me there tomorrow to your *cugino*, Gino?"

"Of course, Gino take you there, tomorrow," he said waving an arm.

The Cozza brothers were parked, waiting in their gold-colored Torino when Magdalena arrived home. The brothers now in their mid-twenties, both men exited their car, well-groomed, albeit in garish silk suits and wearing oily hair products. "*Buona Sera, Senorina,*" both chimed with the utmost respect. "We are here to ask you a question," said Joey, the older brother.

"And what is that?" Magdalena asked with her usual coolness.

Joey smiled. "What is your favorite color?"

Perplexed, Magdalena looked at them both before answering. "Don't you have something better to do than ask such an inane question?"

Shrugging his shoulders, Vinnie said, "I don't know from the word inane. Just what is your favorite color?" Please, Magdalena."

"Maroon. Is that all you need to know?" she said.

Vinnie looked confused.

"Never mind, Vinnie, I know what color she means," Joey told him. And before Magdalena could say more, they were gone.

Chapter 12

Angie took riding lessons at Will Rogers State Park, located in Pacific Palisades. This premier location spoke for itself. Wally Gage, her trainer, produced more winning riders because he stipulated that his students enter horse shows riding talented, expensive mounts. This translated into well-healed clients who paid top dollar for his training. The parents were expected to upgrade their child's horse or horses whenever needed. In turn, these push button steeds, as they came to be named in the horse world, garnered more ribbons for Wally's barn, raising his status and creating proud parents.

For teaching purposes, Wally owned a few barn horses. They were gentle equines, usually older and safe for young riders that he was bringing into his fold. It was a Saturday morning when Angie rode past Wally on a lesson horse. "What are you doing on Goliath?" Wally asked, looking up at Angie, as he pushed a mop of hair from his eyes.

Angie was quick to answer. "He seemed antsy in his stall, and I don't think he has been out for a few days, so I thought I would walk him around."

"Fine with me; he looks happy to be out."

Angie was riding high on Goliath, who was seventeen hands tall. Trotting off down the long barn row, she noted that the top and bottom doors on the last stall in the row were shut. Slowing Goliath to a walk, she approached the enclosure and heard giggles coming from inside. Adjusting the strap of the Polaroid camera around her neck, she gently urged her horse right beside the door. Hands trembling, she carefully pulled on the top door to open it just a crack. Then, leaning forward in her saddle, she adroitly angled the camera to photograph the barn floor. *Swish* went the Polaroid.

Fabulous, thought Angie, they didn't hear the sound of the camera because of their giggling. She took two more photos, holding them in her mouth, until someone pulled the barn door shut. She turned her horse and trotted back to the lesson stalls with a grin as wide as the bit in Goliath's mouth.

*****

Magdalena stared in amazement at the lewd photos of Tracey Manners that Angie tossed on her desk. There was Tracey, without a thread of clothing, having sex with a trainer twice her age on the shavings of the stall floor.

"My god, Angie, how did you get these?" Magdalena said, examining one photo especially close.

"You can thank a very tall horse named, Goliath," Angie said with an impish smile. "I told you she was a slut."

"This was a very cavalier act, Angie. I cannot tell you how surprised I am."

"I don't know what cavalier means, but you can get her and her mother off our backs with these photos, right?"

"Oh yes I can, Angie."

Gathering up the photos as quickly as she had tossed them on Magdalena's desk, Angie demanded, "You can't have them back until you tell me what she did to you."

Privacy drove Magdalena, and she didn't want to share

the intimidating note, even with her sister. The two stared at one another.

"I mean it Em. I shared with you, now you have to do the same with me." Angie stood hands on hips.

With a look of resignation, Magdalena slowly reached for a book above her desk. She flipped through the pages and retrieved the small rolled note written by Tracey. She handed it to Angie.

Angie's eyes narrowed. "I'm not through with her yet," she said tossing the photos back at Magdalena.

"Don't do anything else, Angie. You got information that I can use to create an affidavit that will keep her family away from us forever. I promise."

"That's all legal bullshit. I want more. You just wait and see," Angie said as she marched out of Magdalena's bedroom, slapping her crop against her riding boots.

*****

Gino as promised, drove Magdalena to his cousin's shoe repair shop. The heavy aroma of leather hung in the shop's air. "Gino why you come to my shop? You got no old shoes that need fix!" His cousin said, kidding Gino as he laughed.

"No, I have a young woman needs your help."

With much ceremony, Gino introduced Magdalena. After some friendly dialogue, Magdalena produced the pairs of shoes she wanted altered. Careful measurements were taken and the shoes to be built up were marked.

"One week, I have all your shoes, Miss Magdalena."

When Magdalena left the shoe repair shop, she noticed an antique store nearby. She asked Gino to wait in the truck for her. Stepping into a world she knew little of, she was drawn to a beautiful tea service standing on an elegant tray. It fascinated her. These were the kind of items that belonged in the house where she lived. She ran her fingers over the pieces of the set. In the sugar bowl were tongs fashioned like boney dragon's feet that were burnished in gold. Since she wanted someone in her grip, it seemed just the thing for the occasion she had in mind.

"Ah, I see you've found our *repousse* tea service," the sales lady said. "Not many people serve tea any more. But this early American example is the finest set we have ever had in the shop."

Magdalena nodded. "And what tea cups would you use with it?"

With a spring in her step, the clerk led Magdalena to the back of the store, where antique cup and saucer sets gathered dust. "Now here we have…"

Magdalena interrupted, "I like the ones with rosebuds around the rims. Are those matching plates?"

"Yes, those are cake plates, a set of eight, approximately the same era as the tea set you admired. You have a fine eye."

"I'll take them," Magdalena said.

"The cake plates, cups and saucers?" asked the sales lady.

"And the tea service," added Magdalena.

The sales lady eyed Magdalena more closely then rushed to box the items. Her hand was shaking when she took Magdalena's credit card. Sciacca had put Magdalena on his American Express as a co-signer and told her to use it any time she chose. "This purchase exceeds three hundred dollars. I will have to get an approval."

Magdalena flinched a bit, but nodded and stepped away from the register while the clerk made the call. She took a deep breath and hoped the card would be accepted.

*****

Gino carried the antique shop boxes into the kitchen. "Maria," Magdalena said to the cook. "I want to arrange for a tea for four people next week. I will give you the exact day and time later. Can you make us a cake too?"

"Of course, I can make you a beautiful honey cake with *marzapane*," Maria said while unpacking the items she held up the sugar bowl. "Mama Mia, this looks like things sold out the back door of this house once. *Bella, bella*."

Magdalena saw Angie charge down the stairs in her riding habit, eager to get to the barn. As usual, Gino was outside, in his pick-up truck to drive to her riding lessons. "Angie, can you be here for tea next week?" Magdalena called.

"Tea?" Angie said incredulously. "When did you dream that up?"

"Yes or no Angie! I am inviting Tracey Manners and her mother on Thursday."

Magdalena's words stopped Angie in her tracks. "You bet I'll be there. I'd miss a horse show to be there," she said, forcing a laugh.

"Good, I have a plan that involves your photos."

Romulus and Remus barking excitedly in the garage court interrupted Magdalena and Angie were both drawn outside by the noise. The Cozza bothers stood beside a 1978 Jaguar XKE. The brother's faces held smirks but they said nothing.

"So, you have a new car. Big deal," said Angie to the Cozza brothers as she walked around the maroon colored sports car secretly loving it.

Magdalena stood back watching the brothers. They looked smug.

When Joey opened the door on the driver's side, sweeping his arm toward Magdalena, Angie's squeal shattered the air.

Magdalena calmly walked toward Joey Cozza. “Is this car from my father for my birthday?” Magdalena asked, with controlled excitement.

“You could say that,” Joey said.

Chapter 13

Originally, Del did not care to be chauffeured in the limousine Sciacca had made available for him. It screamed Mob to him and he used it only for court appearances in Los Angeles when absolutely necessary. But his Corvair was getting old, and he was beginning to let Alberto drive him in the big car on certain occasions.

He had become adept at avoiding trial work, showing up in court for important cases or final argument only. And a new breed of lawyer was emerging to do appearance work. Del hired them for arraignments, and motions, and default hearings. Like most criminal lawyers, Del sidestepped court. Defending gangsters was tough, but when the judge and jury actually saw patently guilty clients, pleading their cases was twice as difficult.

Del's aim in court was for a quiet and respectful demeanor, wearing expensive but understated attire. Nevertheless, everyone knew he was a well-paid mouthpiece for the Mafia. Relief always swept over him when he left the courtroom.

As Del exited the long corridor of the Federal court building after a rare appearance, an ex-colleague from the San Francisco D.A.'s office caught his eye. "McGuire," Del called from across the hall. "How in the hell are you? It's been a long time." Del walked briskly toward the man with his hand outstretched.

McGuire's head spun in Del's direction, then scorn flashed across his face. "Yeah, not long enough, D'Alessandro," McGuire retorted. "How does it feel working the other side of the street dressed up like a pimp in your silk shirts?"

Del's forward movement halted as he dropped his hand and his jaw.

*****

The following day, Del received a call from Sciacca to meet him at the Bel Air for lunch. Del had Alberto drive him the short distance to the hotel.

Sciacca had taken to this charming hideaway where the service was exceptional. He would never admit it, but it excited him that movie stars frequented the place. Sciacca also asked for meetings of special importance here when he didn't want to use the phone. He endeavored to make life easy for D'Alessandro, ever since the beating of Magdalena took from 'that *goniff,'* a word Sciacca borrowed from the Yiddish that defined thief.

When Del arrived at the hotel, he made the call from the lobby to Sciacca's bungalow. "D'Alessandro," Sciacca answered cheerfully. "Do you know what day this is?" He continued without waiting for an answer. "It's Magdalena's birthday!"

Del winced at the fact that he had forgotten, and that Sciacca even knew the date. "I… I was just about to call her," he answered defensively.

"Yeah, call her. But I wanted you to know that I took care of her gift, and she thinks it's from you, of course."

Indignation consumed Del. "Sciacca, I am perfectly capable of buying a birthday gift for my daughter."

"And you just did, Del. You know, when a girl reaches eighteen, she should have a car. I had the Cozza boys deliver it today. When you call her, see how she likes it?"

Del sighed. "Okay, thanks, I guess."

Sciacca continued, "Now, I want to talk to you about a guy who has been arrested. He's at LAX being held by the feds. You have to meet with him there before ten a.m. so just stay at the hotel tonight and have your guy, Alberto come by for you in the morning. We'll talk about it in the Garden Room for lunch. You won't believe their tortilla soup!"

*****

Oh great, Papa is away and I can use his office to prepare my document. With the Manners' coming to tea, the next day, Magdalena felt confident about her plan. She reached for a folder and placed the document she had prepared, along with the revealing photos of Tracey having sex with a trainer in a horse stall. The paperwork consisted of an agreement that the Manner's family would never denigrate the D'Alessandro family again. She knew the photos would force Mrs. Manners to sign it. Magdalena sat in her father's office chair with a wry smile and conspiracy in her eyes, thinking about the tea.

She got up and went to the kitchen. "Maria will you be ready for our tea tomorrow?" She said, running her fingers around the silver tray holding the tea service.

Maria looked puzzled. "Yes, tomorrow you say I make tea and cake, and I will make tea and cake."

"But do you have everything you need?"

"Yes. You no worry, Magdalena. I will even dress nice when I serve you."

"Really? That would be lovely."

Maria stood drying her hands on a dishtowel. "She has

more than this tea in her head," Maria muttered.

The following day, Angie was up early and barged into Magdalena's room in her riding gear. "I'm going to the barn, Em, but I'll be back for the Manners teatime bullshit."

"You'd better be," Magdalena said, sitting up in bed.

"Isn't it neat that you can park the Jag right in front of the house for Tracy and her mother to drool over."

Magdalena nodded with a sly smile. "I have to take driving lessons with Alberto and get my driving license before I can take it out on the street, but I had him park it right in the middle of the garage court for tomorrow's tea."

Chapter 14

The Manner's Lincoln Continental hummed up the winding drive to the house. "I had no idea this property was so large. We must have passed a hundred oleander bushes along this gorgeous driveway," Mrs. Manners said.

"Are you sure we're at the right house, Mother?" asked Tracey.

"Of course, I'm sure. I once met the family that lived here. They were wealthy Germans with silver mines in Mexico. This D'Alessandro bunch, however, works for the Mafia. We'll never return, but I wanted to see the inside of the house just once."

Tracey squirmed in her car seat. "What's the Mafia?"

"Oh, for heaven's sake, look it up in our encyclopedia."

"Well, I wish we hadn't come. I have a strange feeling about being here."

"Don't be silly. Oh look, there's a man to direct us where to park."

Tracey's eyes bulged. "Oh my god, look at that Jag, Mother."

"Yes, look at it. Rather gauche of the father to drive such a racy car."

Gino, with cap in hand, subserviently opened Mrs. Manner's passenger door.

Magdalena met them at the entrance, cool and polite, she welcomed them and directed them toward the living room. "Sorry, I left my Jag there in the way. It probably is harder for you to park."

Tracey emitted a faint whimper.

As the women walked across the large anteroom, tiled in black and white marble, they couldn't find words to acknowledge Magdalena's Jaguar. Instead they flashed surprised expressions at one another mixed with envy. But Mrs. Manners was soon distracted as she gawked upward at the high-coffered ceiling and serpentine staircase. Magdalena hid her grin.

The pair of mastiffs lounged on the cool floor, and looked up with mild curiosity at the passing women.

"My, those are huge dogs! Are they safe?" asked Mrs. Manners as she adjusted her mink stole around her shoulders.

"Aren't they beauties?" Angie said, laughing as she came in. She quickened her step to follow Mrs. Manners and Tracey. "They just had their annual checkup and weighed in at one hundred-seventy-five pounds, each. But don't worry, they're harmless and the kindest dogs you'll ever know. Of course, thy would do anything to protect our family."

"Are you having tea in riding attire, Angelina?" Mrs. Manners circled around the mastiffs frowning.

"Yep, I'm in britches and boots whenever possible."

After the four women had settled themselves in the living room, an awkward silence followed. Magdalena turned to Angie. "Would you ask Maria to serve us tea, Angie?"

Angie's eyes rolled, but she did as her sister asked and headed toward the kitchen.

Maria soon entered with the gleaming tea service, an enticing cake decorated with almonds and a large dish of peanut butter cookies. When she lowered the tray before them Magdalena saw she wore a shiny grey uniform with an organdy apron. Angie covered a grin. Magdalena could see that Mrs. Manners was impressed with the antique tea set.

"Far out, Maria, you made peanut butter cookies, too," Angie said as she grabbed one.

Magdalena frowned at Angie.

"Ah… try these cookies, Tracey," Angie said with a mouthful, "they're super."

After a brief discussion of horse shows, and some polite exchanges about the tea, the conversation grew idle among the four women.

Magdalena reached for her folder.

With a wide grin Angie straightened in her chair.

"I invited you here, Mrs. Manners, to show you some photographs, and ask that you sign this document."

"What did you say," Mrs. Manners appeared bemused.

"Please look at these photographs, and you will see why your signature is required on this agreement so you may never…

"Oh no!" Tracey said, as she grabbed the photos from her mother.

Magdalena continued, "You and your daughter will no longer defame this family, Mrs. Manners, or I will release these to the local press."

"And, Tracey will no longer write anonymous notes calling my sister a gimpy wop," fired Angie.

An affronted Mrs. Manners' jaw dropped when she took the photos from Tracey and viewed them. "Why I never…"

"Just sign the document, Manners," Angie said, "Or my sister *will* do what she says. Believe me."

Outrage and astonishment inflamed Mrs. Manners face. After scribbling her signature on the document, she pushed her daughter from the room towards the entry. Passing Romulus and Remus in haste, Mrs. Manners let her wrap slip from her arm and drag on the entry floor. Romulus settled a huge paw on that end of the mink cape, leaving her pulling on the other end. With a mixture of horror and fear, Mrs. Manners desperately tugged at her fur. "You brutes, give me my stole," she managed to whimper.

Misinterpreting their play, she dropped her mink wrap, and scrambled for the door. Arriving at her vehicle, she had trouble starting it. Hitting the starter, a second time, evoked an excruciating metal sound that brought the dogs to the car, barking. The Lincoln Continental jerked, and chugged sporadically down the drive, with Mrs. Manners swearing all the way.

*****

On the drive home from LAX, Del was embarrassed that he had forgotten Magdalena's birthday. As he stared out the car window, his face was drawn and immobile. Today, the accumulated anxiety from the years he'd spent with 'The Family,' seemed more repugnant than usual. For a moment, his vision blurred. He rubbed his eyes and blinked several times. He slid the frame of his reading glasses back to his eyes, and guessed it was time to visit his optometrist.

Turning to his briefcase, he sighed. For diversion, he decided to take a look at the case file on the client he'd interviewed at the airport. The man had been transporting several kilos of cocaine from the interior of Mexico, where he was arrested at the Tijuana border. Narcotics were becoming more and more a part of Del's caseload, most of the drugs coming from Mexico. The man was a small-time thug who had gotten in over his head. Sciacca had told Del to sacrifice the guy, let him "take the fall." That would not be difficult for Del, but Sciacca had said something that disturbed him to his core. 'I want you to get the punk's connection in Mexico.'

Setting the paperwork aside to gaze out the car window again, Del said aloud, "Jesus, what the hell is happening to client confidentiality?" He absently rubbed his left leg, disgusted at the new element of narcotics creeping into his already sullied practice.

A sharp headache struck him. He wanted to get home, *he needed a brandy and a couple of Anacin.* That would ease his pain. His thoughts wandered to Magdalena. He realized he didn't even know what kind of a car he had supposedly given her.

The light of day had slipped away by the time the limousine came to a stop in the garage court. Del tried to exit the vehicle on his own but couldn't. His left leg wouldn't support him. Alberto had to help D'Alessandro into the house and up to his bedroom.

Chapter 15

Magdalena knocked on her father's bedroom door before entering. She wanted to say good morning and welcome him home from Los Angeles. He might want to sleep in, but she had exciting news. Of course, she wanted to thank him for her beautiful new car and make him think she believed he had given her the Jaguar, even though she suspected Sciacca had planned it all. Briefly, she thought she might even relate the triumphant outcome of her tea party, then decided against it.

But the letter she had received in the morning mail took precedence over everything. UCLA had granted her admission, based on her high SAT scores and her 4.0 grade average at St Mary's. Without waiting for her father to answer, she entered his bedroom to find the room dark. It was ten a.m. and the blackout curtains were still closed.

"Papa," Magdalena called. When she received no answer, she went to his bed and took his hand. It felt clammy. "Wake up Papa." She felt his forehead and spoke to him again, still with no response. She walked to the window and yanked open one of the heavy, black drapes. In the bright sun light his face lay gray on his pillow. She ran from the bedroom, leaned over the staircase railing and yelled, "Maria, get Alberto. "Come quick!"

*****

On the ambulance ride to the hospital, Magdalena queried the attendant about her father's condition. If her father were able to speak, the oxygen mask on his face prevented her from responding. She held his hand tightly. *Did he just squeeze back a little?* She wondered. *Papa looks so tired, so drawn and has aged a great deal in just a few days.*

At the hospital, Magdalena tried to follow the gurney being wheeled into the emergency entrance but a staff member diverted her to a crowded waiting room.

She sat rigid and silent when Angelina arrived, followed by Alberto. "Em, do you think Daddy will die?" Angie had lapsed into acting much younger that her fourteen years. "No, Angie I don't." Magdalena watched her sister who she knew was about to explode. "Why don't you get us some hot chocolate from the machine?"

"I don't want any hot chocolate! I want to know if Daddy will live. Why can't someone come and talk to us?"

"Angelina! People are looking at us. Don't shout. Sit down," Magdalena said trying to sound calm. "We just have to wait for the doctor. I'm going to the restroom. Wait here."

Magdalena stepped into a bathroom stall, shut the door and vomited green bile. When her retching was done, she washed her face and rinsed her mouth. She leaned over the sink to examine herself in the mirror. She looked composed. *If necessary, I will be the head of this family, with the help of Sciacca and my law degree. I must be in control, not emotional like Angie.* Magdalena checked her facial expression again so as to assure herself that she looked poised, before returning to the reception area.

"How can you be so calm? What if Daddy dies, then we will be orphans," blurted Angie.

A tall, narrow-faced man with pocked skin and greying hair strode into the waiting room. His custom- tailored, dark suit and shirt were accented by a white tie. He inquired at reception about Dominic D'Alessandro.

Magdalena stared up at the man. As she met his eyes she knew it was Sciacca, despite never having met him. He took a seat next to her. "What can I do, Magdalena?"

Magdalena knew Sciacca's confident voice. They had talked on the phone. She had kept this communication and their notes clandestine, knowing that her father would be further wounded if he knew.

Magdalena shook her head and looked at Sciacca. "We are just waiting for the doctor to tell us how bad Papa is."

He read the worry in her eyes. "I will find the best specialist in L.A. and fly him here. Don't you worry. I want you to consider me your secret godfather," Sciacca said as he patted her hand, his eyes showing his approval of her Italian beauty.

Frowning, Angelina approached them. "Who are you?" she asked.

"Angelina, this is Mr. Sciacca, the man Papa is employed by."

Sciacca stood and held out both his hands to Angie, who ignored them.

"Oh, the Family boss. You got here quick."

"Angie, please sit down and don't be so rude to Mr. Sciacca."

"This is a tough time, Angie. I understand," Sciacca said.

A doctor walked toward them and they fell silent. "Hello, I'm Dr. Weeks," he said to Magdalena. Your father is resting quietly and is in no pain, but he *has* suffered a stroke."

Magdalena stood and nodded.

"It appears that his left side will be paralyzed to some degree. In a few days, we'll be able to assess whether he's suffered cognitive loss."

"What is cognitive loss?" blurted Angie.

"That would be, a deterioration of his mental activity."

"Oh, poor Daddy!" cried Angie, letting her tears flow.

"But I want to stress that we don't have a complete prognosis yet. With today's physical therapy and blood pressure medications, his paralysis may diminish substantially."

Sciacca cleared his throat, stood, and appeared to take charge. "I will have the top stroke doctor here within hours. Is there someone you can recommend, Doctor?"

Over his magnifying glasses, Doctor Weeks viewed the tall man with curiosity, "May I ask who you are, Sir?"

"He is a close friend of the family," Magdalena interjected.

"Well, ah, there is a doctor in Beverly Hills who practices at Cedars Sinai Hospital. He is the most respected man in the field of hemorrhagic strokes."

"Then that's who we want. What is his name?" asked Sciacca.

The doctor removed his glasses, dumbfounded. "You can't think that you could persuade Doctor Fine to just drop his practice and come here?"

"That's exactly what I plan," Sciacca said. When he turned to Magdalena to say goodbye, he gave her a kiss on the check, and was about to do the same to Angie.

"Save it," Angie said, with an upheld hand.

Sciacca spoke softly, "Don't worry, Magdalena, I'll take care of this," he said heading toward the exit.

Two days later in Doctor Week's examining room, his

nurse spoke through the intercom. "You have a call from a Doctor Fine."

Weeks looked surprised. "David Fine?"

"I didn't ask his first name but I think it is the specialist I've heard you…"

"Never mind," Weeks said as he rushed to his office telephone leaving his patient behind.

The conversation with Fine lasted but a minute. Week's held the phone receiver for a long moment after the call had ended. "Nurse," he called, "clear my afternoon schedule."

Within the hour, the two doctors were introducing themselves by their first names and expressing professional respect for one another. Fine was the older of the two men, conservatively dressed and formal in demeanor.

After Fine had examined D'Alessandro at his bedside and reviewed his chart, both doctors retired to Week's office.

"It appears that you have done all that was possible for the patient. At this stage, he is clearly ready to leave the hospital. The medications you have prescribed along with physical therapy are exactly the course I would have taken," Fine said.

"I am curious, David, what persuaded you to consult on this somewhat garden variety stroke?"

"Yes, well let's just say that a rather large donation was made to our cardiovascular unit at Cedars by this gentleman, Jimmy Sciacca."

Week's eyebrows rose, "I don't even know who this Sciacca is or what business he is in. Do you?"

"I did have my lawyer look into his history and found that he is in many business, most of them underground, if you know what I mean. Your patient, D'Alessandro, is his indispensable lawyer and handles all of his legal work."

Weeks looked surprised. After pausing for a moment to understand what had just been said, he nodded. "Ah, I see. Well, I'm glad you got a donation from his ill-gotten profits for your time and the cardiovascular unit."

"Yes, and with this man's resources, you may well be pleased that you didn't lose your patient."

With a dry smile, Weeks sat contemplating that thought.

Chapter 16

Even though it was a sad drive home, Alberto was proud as he drove Del and Magdalena home from the hospital. His past job had included chauffeuring, so he was at home driving people, especially when formally dressed. Now he was no longer referred to as the housekeeper's husband. On occasion, Angie recruited him to haul her trainer's horse van from her boarding facility at Will Rogers State Park to local shows. Alberto always dressed neatly on those occasions, but hanging in his closet, ready for use, was his chauffeur's uniform and cap that he now wore.

When the limousine arrived in the garage court, Magdalena stepped quickly to her father's side of the car. Alberto walked to the entry where the new electric wheelchair was parked. Magdalena had arranged for the purchase of the chair with the help of Sciacca. As Alberto's long arms settled the chair beside the opened car door, the wheels made crunching sounds on the gravel. "Mr. D'Alessandro, I will help you."

In the back seat of the limousine, Del looked smaller to Magdalena and his speaking seemed difficult. His words were indistinct as he tried to say something to Alberto.

"I think my father wants you to call him, Del, not 'Mr. D'Alessandro,'" Magdalena said.

"Yes, Mr. Del," answered Alberto with the habitual bow reflecting his many years in domestic service.

"Watisiss?" Del said, pointing at the new chair.

"This is the wheelchair that was recommended for you, Papa, Magdalena said, avoiding Sciacca's involvement.

Alberto tried to sound cheerful. "Yes, this one has buttons for you to drive it. It will be much easier to use than the one I had when I come home from the hospital, Mr. Del."

One side of Del's face worked, the other was set with a grim look.

Gino came running up the driveway calling and waving his cap. "You back Mr. Del; you back," out of breath.

Magdalena acknowledged him. "Help Alberto with my father, please, Gino."

"Yes, yes I help."

While the two men assisted had her father into the chair, Magdalena watched the dogs rally around him, their tails whipped furiously. The mastiff's huge heads came to rest on his lap. Both men stopped moving Del forward while the dogs showed their joy at his return. Magdalena could see they were using all their restraint not to jump up on her father.

"They know he sick, Alberto," Gino said quietly, his eyes feeling with tears.

Alberto nodded.

Del touch the dogs' massive heads. In return, their expressive eyes delivered that special devotion only canines have.

Once in the house, Magdalena saw her father gaze up at the grand staircase. She suspected he was wondering if he would ever ascend these stairs again. Magdalena took the chair from Alberto and wheeled her father into his office with Romulus and Remus following.

"New?" Del said, pointing to a leather couch.

"Yes, Papa, it makes into a bed. You can sleep down here for now. Does it feel good to be home?" She said as she bent down to kiss his check.

When Del nodded it was with tears running down his cheeks. "Good. Dif-fer-ent."

"Remember the nurse at the hospital, Papa? She said that after a near death experience, people often have different feelings about things."

Del nodded.

Once behind his desk, Del turned in his chair to peck on his typewriter: a-n-g-e-l-i-n-a?

"She is on her way home from the barn, Papa."

Then her father typed, M-a-r-i-a.

Magdalena called for Maria.

The knock on the door brought throaty growls from the dogs until Maria's entrance.

"*Buongiorno*, Maria," Del tried to say but the words didn't come out well, so Del's fingers went back to the typewriter to spell S-A-U-S-A-G-E-S and P-E-P…

Magdalena interrupted him with a touch on his shoulder. "Maria, Papa wants sausage and peppers for dinner. He missed your wonderful cooking after a week of hospital food."

A huge smile crossed Maria's face. "I make. And good you are home," she said, drying her eyes with the hem of her apron. Maria was an accomplished cook and knew it. But, the look on her face said, it was good to be told so.

Another knock to the door, and this time Magdalena heard her father speak in a strong voice. "Come."

Rosella stood in the office doorway, looking sad. Rosella had, not too long ago, seen a stalwart man reduced to a wheelchair. "We are all happy you are home and well, Mr. Del," she said. Everyone knew Alberto had been in a wheel chair for months after the attack on Magdalena.

Del nodded to Rosella, "*Grazie*."

The one-word comments were coming clear, Magdalena thought, gratefully.

Rosella shuffled her feet and wrung her hands. "You know Alberto and I are *grato* to be here. You gave us a home."

Del's left arm made only a slight move. Magdalena watched him defer to his right and wave Rosella's comment away.

"May I ask something?" Rosella said, still wringing her hands, looking at Magdalena and then her father.

Del nodded.

It was clear Rosella had difficulty asking her question.

"Is there a problem, Maria?" Magdalena asked.

"No, it's just that Alberto want to help you as *valetto*."

Magdalena saw her father's questioning look at the use of the word.

"You know, like a manservant," Rosella said. "He used to do that."

Sitting back in his chair, Del produced his lop-sided smile, and nodded.

*****

In a short time, everyone heard Angie's hooping for joy outside when she learned her father was home. Magdalena paused to watch Angie charge toward the entrance, the sound of her riding boots clumping on the marble floor like the hooves of a horse. "Oh Daddy, I'm so glad you're home," she said, coming to a skidding halt at his door before running to him. When she pounced on his lap, the wheelchair nearly toppled and they both laughed.

Angelina was her father's only focus. Everyone else was forgotten. Magdalena stepped from his office. Peering back briefly, she saw Angie throw her arms around her father and give him a giant hug.

"Your, your hair," Del said as he smelled and stroked Angie's ponytail.

"Maria says it's the color of her biscotti," Angelina proudly announced.

With his crocked grin, Del smiled and nodded.

Magdalena thought, *Angie arrives with the smell of alfalfa hay and sweat. Her light skin and hair coloring must have come from the north of Italy, on Mama's side. I have Papa's olive skin and black hair.* Magdalena stepped away from the door opening, but stood to listen, unseen.

"Oh, Daddy," Angie said, "I have great news. I already told Magdalena and Maria, but I am supposed to wait for dinner to surprise you."

"Tell!" Del said, struggling to match her enthusiasm.

"But I said I would wait."

"Tell!" Del said growing more eager.

"I have been invited to train with the Junior Olympic Team! But Daddy, it means that you have to buy me very expensive horses, at least two, and they will cost maybe $25,000 dollars each."

"I buy, Champ-i-on-essa," he said, speaking as clearly as he had spoken all afternoon.

"Really?" She said, with an exuberance that Magdalena knew warmed Papa's heart.

Outside, in the corridor, Magdalena leaned against the wall as envy washed over her. *I know this feeling isn't right, but after all I am the one who takes care of papa. I am just not the one who looks like mama. Angie will leave Papa someday. I will never leave.*

Magdalena trudged up the stairs to her room, where she placed a vinyl record on the turntable: Piano Concerto Number 2 in C Minor, Opus 18 Composer Rachmaninoff. The music was rich and stirring, exuding happiness then sadness, just like parts of her life. She found the pounding and almost violent parts to her liking. It defined how she felt but never revealed.

Chapter 17

Paola appeared at the door one day. Magdalena had just returned from a class at UCLA. "Paola, it is so good to see you! Where have you been?" She remembered her father had taken Paola to the local convent where she had been provided with a room. It had been a rather mysterious move, and Magdalena never really understood Paola's story.

Her cousin looked different, less alive and outgoing. She wore a plain grey dress that was more like a uniform, pinned with a nametag. Why does her name tag say Mancuso? Magdalena wondered, Paola isn't married.

"Angie is riding horses at the barn, and papa is away. Come into the kitchen for a cup of espresso."

Paola settled herself at the round kitchen table. "You go to the school of law soon, Magdalena, like your father?"

"Yes, I'm just about to finish my senior year at UCLA, and then I will go to Loyola Law School here in Los Angeles, instead of USF, like Papa. I am anxious to assist him when I have my law degree." I will be able to help papa." Magdalena was trying to keep her phrases simple for Paola, but her aunt's expression was blank, as though she was elsewhere. "I notice your name tag says Mancuso. Is that a name you use at the convent?"

Paola then spoke out of context. "It was when he went

to his law school in San Francisco that he changed."

"What do you mean, changed?" Magdalena thought Paola meant that her father's work for the Organization or possibly his stroke had changed him.

"When he changed his name from Mancuso to D'Alessandro," Paola said.

Magdalena asked, "When exactly was that, Paola?" She felt stupid for no knowing that Mancuso was Paola's last name, but was it *her own* family name?

Paola fidgeted with her worn black purse. "Papa Del became fancy in law school about a lot of things. After he married your mother, god rest her soul, he changed. He liked to show her around because she was *bionda.* And that's when he changed his name from Mancuso. It is a name that came from the big island, SiSi…"

"Sicily." Magdalena confirmed.

"A bad name, Mancuso, I heard him say, a name from *Cosa Nostra.*" He did not want people to think he was related to them. But it is my name, I keep.

*****

Angelina was thrilled to leave St Mary's and join the Junior Olympic Equestrian Team. This became a great tonic for Magdalena's father, and he showed great pride in her successes. If nothing else, it improved his speech as he labored to communicate her successes. He remained in his wheelchair but entered a new phase of life. Magdalena was equally happy to enter Loyola University. She thought her father was complacent about his practice after his stroke. It seemed sad that it took such a near fatal event to bring him contentment. Still, she felt he was doing something clandestine, though she never found any paperwork to confirm her suspicions. He had fooled her once before, and she felt sure it was happening again.

*****

In the following years, Magdalena finally felt her father had decided to stay in their beautiful villa with the elegant pool. She was always grateful for the ability to swim daily. When they were poor in Little Italy at their grandparent's flat, she had walked six blocks to the public pool. Now, swimming was but a few steps away - her exercise, her pleasure, and her solace.

One day, as she stood drying her hair after a morning swim, Magdalena heard the elevator activate. That would be her father and his physical therapist. Del now used the pool, and the elevator allowed him to arrive in his wheelchair. When the door opened someone new wheeled her father's chair out onto the pool deck.

"Hello, I'm Lance Otis," your father's new physical therapist," said the confident, tanned young man in Hawaiian trunks. He looked like he belonged on a beach, not poolside indoors.

After Lance jumped towards her to shake her hand, she saw his eyes linger on her shorter leg. She felt vulnerable, and scrambled to put on her long terry cloth robe.

"Would you like to stay and see how your father is doing?" Lance said brushing a mop of blond hair from his brow.

She couldn't help but notice his long, lean handsome physique. "I can't this morning," she said, avoiding his inquisitive pale blue eyes. She turned to her father. "Papa, I am interviewing the lawyer we talked about at the house yesterday."

Del nodded. "My daughter is about to finish law school," he said clearly, owing to his speech therapist. It was the first time she remembered her father ever praising her, although his comment was delivered more as a matter of fact than a compliment.

Magdalena dashed to her room, showered and dressed for the interview. She rushed down the stairs, pausing to meet Lance again in the foyer. Dressed, he even looked taller, like an ad for a surfboard. His appraisal of her was long and bold. In her maroon pantsuit, with bellbottoms covering her corrected shoe, she felt more confident.

Lance stepped toward her. "Your father will do better, now that I'm his therapist.

"Really," Magdalena said in her aloof style.

"Yeah, really." Lance grinned broadly. "The guy who was working with him before is a wimp. Sorry to say, but I am much better."

"Okay, I'll wait and see," Magdalena said, walking toward her father's office. When she turned to close the door, she saw Lance standing perfectly still, staring at her with a cocky smile.

"Magdalena."

"Yes?"

"How about I pick you up Friday night and we see a great surfing movie, then go for some burgers?"

A great surfing movie, gee, just what I have always wanted to see.

"Okay." *Why did I say that*?

*****

Once she passed the bar, Magdalena planned to sit as her father's second chair. With care, she would convince him it would be for a short time only. But she knew she had to slowly take over the practice. She also knew Sciacca expected this, and the idea excited her. Because she didn't carry the shame her father did about working for the Organization, she felt sure she could do as good a job, maybe better. Sciacca would have to find someone, and she was eminently qualified. Further, it would be a well-paying position that she needed, as she would ultimately be responsible for the family income. What concerned her was how to tell her father. She decided she would just wait and see how it played out.

Magdalena walked into the office and saw Michael Tynan standing next to the file cabinet near the window. He seemed nervous, and when offered, quickly took a seat in front of her father's desk. "I… I was admiring the beautiful view you have of the outside patio," he said.

Magdalena nodded, taking a seat in her father's high-backed leather chair. She observed Tynan across from her. The ensuing silence seemed difficult for him, and she thought she saw him squirm, just a little. "Mr. Tynan, do you have a problem being hired by a woman?"

He looked relieved at her comment. "No. No not at all.

"Alright," Magdalena said with a minimal smile. "Let me be candid with you, Mr. Tynan. My father has been in therapy for years. During much of that time, we have managed to hire appearance lawyers for court. But his caseload is backing up and briefs need to be written, as well as other details that a law office has to deal with. I'm sure you understand."

Tynan nodded, with attentive interest. "Of course.

"I have been able to help him with some of the work, but because I am still in law school, I haven't had the time to keep up with all of it."

"Certainly, I believe I could be of great help to you and your father. You've seen my resume. I've done this kind of work before."

"Yes, but only for about a year. Why did you leave?" Magdalena knew the answer: the firm had moved to Chicago. She suspected Tynan hadn't wanted to relocate, even though the company had invited him to join them. Magdalena had already called his references, and they were excellent.

Tynan explained what she already knew, and together they reviewed his education at Catholic schools, as well as UCLA and Loyola Law. His education closely resembled hers. "Your education will make my father happy," Magdalena said. "It's almost too perfect."

Magdalena thought she saw that slight squirm again in Tynan. Her immediate response was to be suspicious, but she let the feeling go.

Magdalena's cool manner made her appear aloof, yet she wanted to be specific about the position and what she expected from Tynan. "Your experience in this field has been short, Mr. Tynan. This is a criminal law practice exclusively, and you need to understand we are defending types that offend many lawyers, and judges. You must decide now if this could become a problem." What Magdalena failed to mention was that all of their cases were guilty, and everyone they defended was a member of the Organization.

"I understand that, Miss D'Alessandro, and I'm looking forward to working with you and your father," Tynan said, looking into her dark eyes.

She shook Tynan's hand and walked him to the door. "My father and I will expect you at nine a.m., Monday morning," she said with a token smile.

After Tynan was gone, she remained at her father's oversized desk, tapping her pen on a yellow pad. Having accepted a date with Lance made her think of something long overdue.

Chapter 18

Magdalena told the receptionist, “Hello, I’m Maggie Mancuso. I called earlier this morning.” She had planned on using a false name, and this one came immediately to mind. She would do some research on the name in the near future but for now, it was amusing to use the name Paola said was their real surname.

Magdalena was led into the doctor’s office, where she sat and waited about fifteen minutes. She was about to leave when the doctor entered.

“Hello, Miss Mancuso. My, you resemble that Italian movie star, I can’t quite remember her name.”

“Yes, people have told me that before,” she said. She knew he referred to Sophia Loren, but wanting no chitchat, she delved into her story.

The doctor’s response was one of surprise. “This is an unusual request, Miss Mancuso. I am curious to know what your motivation is for this procedure?” he asked.

“Do I have to give you one?”

“No, not necessarily, but I am wondering if fear of having intercourse is perhaps the reason. I can recommend a fine psychologist that could help clear any anxieties you may have about your first sexual experience.”

Magdalena was ready for this question and had

rehearsed her answer, false though it was. She spoke slowly and clearly. "My mother told me that the women in our family have suffered greatly the first time they had sex because of an abnormally thick hymen." Her face bore no emotion as she continued. "She said she wished she could have gone to a doctor ahead of her wedding night to correct the problem, but women didn't do those things then." Magdalena sat back in her chair, wondering if he bought her story. *He can't begin to understand that I will have no man thinking I am his virginal conquest.*

"I see. Well, I guess I was wondering if you had been listening to that Gloria Steinem woman who promotes some radical ideas about sex."

"Doctor, I am about to finish my senior year at UCLA. I just haven't had time for sex. But now that I can see it is about to happen, I want this done. Can you please help me? *I should have probably gone to a woman doctor. I'm leaving if he wants any more explanations.*

"Yes, I believe I understand. But have you thought what you will tell the young man in this situation?"

Magdalena could see that the doctor was still struggling with the virgin issue. She hated saying what came out next, but she wanted this procedure now. "Perhaps I could refer him to you if he has any questions about my virginity." Her cool demeanor nearly thawed as she repressed a smile, at the thought of Lance having any questions about her virginity. "Just one other thing, Doctor, I would like a prescription for the pill that prevents pregnancy."

Leaving the doctor's office, after making an appointment for the procedure, Magdalena mulled over the fact that she *was* different, abnormal some would say for wanting this. But giving up control was against her uncommon feelings. She would likely have sex with Lance and many other men in her lifetime. What she would never do is marry. Her marriage would forever be to her father, her family and her profession. She had sworn that to the Virgin Mary when she was fourteen.

*****

Angie took the stairs two at a time, then barged into Magdalena's bedroom. "I want to go to Hawaii! Everyone from the barn is going for a month this summer."

"Angie, could you knock once in a while?"

"Please, Em, if you don't say yes, I am going to Daddy. I just wanted to ask you first because I know you have taken over everything including hiring that new hunk as Daddy's physical therapist."

"That wasn't my decision, it was his doctor's."

"Well, I'd shag him."

"It's nice to see you have dropped the F-word, Angie. Growing up a bit?"

"No, I still like the F-word, but there is a new rider at the barn that uses 'shag.' She's from England, and I like the word. But let's get back to Hawaii, Em. I really want to go!"

"You're just eighteen, Angie."

"Big deal, so?"

Magdalena sighed, "I'll talk to Papa." She added, but you have to get me some chaperone names and tell me where you'll be staying."

"No problem, I'll have all that stuff for you by tonight," She darted away.

*****

Angie sat chatting in the kitchen with Maria, enthusiastically rambling on about going to Hawaii for a vacation, when the doorbell sounded. When Angie left to answer the door, a troubled look crossed the cook's face. Hearing that *her* Angelina was going to Hawaii troubled

Maria.

After opening the front door, Angie had difficulty containing her excitement. This was Lance, the hunk she had described to all her girlfriends at the barn. "Cool Hawaiian shirt," she told him. "I love the surfboards," she added, running her finger over the designs on his shirt.

"Thanks. You're the little sister, right?" Lance said, his eyes brightening Angie's smile.

"Yeah, but not too little to go surfing with you."

Magdalena descended the stairs in a white pantsuit, annoyed to find Angie flirting with Lance.

Angie said, "So, are you guys going someplace interesting, like a dark beach?"

Magdalena narrowed her eyes with a dead stare. "Angie, you wanted me to talk to papa about Hawaii?"

Angie backed off, wiggling her fingers in goodbye.

Magdalena turned away, "I'll be right there Lance, I just want to say goodnight to my father," she said turning toward his office and stepping abruptly.

*****

The ride to the theatre reminded her of riding with Gino. Lance's truck was a little newer, but a nevertheless a truck for hauling his surfboards. She had dressed a little too nicely for this very informal event. *Why hadn't I known that?*

Magdalena soon found herself sitting in a small, crowded movie theatre filled with men. It was an art house in Venice, a fancy name for a rundown theatre that showed offbeat films. Lance bought a bucket of popcorn, and sat like a little kid waiting for the screening to begin. The first few riders in the surfing film were pretty spectacular. But Magdalena soon found all the rides melding into one, even with Lance's enthusiastic narration. Bent on describing each ride and who was who in the film, his voice became louder and more animated until someone behind him called out, “Keep it down. Save it, man!” Magdalena watched Lance tense up as he turned around. “You got a problem with me, we can take it outside.”

“Yeah, dickhead, let’s!” The two huffed and puffed their way toward the exit. Magdalena thought she could almost smell the scent of testosterone in the air.

With the absence of Lance the theatre audience quieted down, and Magdalena slipped out to the lobby. She located the manager and asked him to call her a cab.

“I don’t blame you for leaving,” the manager said. “They’re both down the street duking it out in the alley. You must be very upset.”

Magdalena had made a foolish mistake by accepting the blond Neanderthal’s invitation. A moment of chemistry between two people did not make a relationship, nor in this case, a date. Clearly the only attraction Lance had was his good looks. She wouldn’t make such a mistake again.

While Magdalena waited for her cab, she asked for a telephone book and looked up the famous diner, *The Apple Pan*, where the burgers were time honored specialties. Movies stars were known to send chauffeurs there for orders to go. Magdalena had decided to have her cab stop there and order burgers to take home for her and Angie. There would be no way to avoid Angie’s questions when she came home early from her date with Lance.

When the cab pulled into the garage court and Magdalena stepped from the taxi, Angie was there in a minute. “What happened, did you hate him? Did you have a fight? He really isn’t your type, you know.”

“You’re right, he really isn’t my type, Angie.”

“I smell fries.”

Magdalena nodded, "I brought back an order from the *Apple Pan*. Let's go upstairs to my room."

With their spread of cheeseburgers and fries on the floor, Magdalena initiated a long-overdue conversation. "Angie, have you had sex yet?"

"Yeah. Why? Haven't you?"

Magdalena concealed her surprise. "I just wondered with you going to Hawaii and all."

"YOU MEAN I CAN GO!" Angie yelled, tossing down her burger and reaching for Magdalena.

"Yes, Daddy says his *championessa* deserves a vacation for being invited to join the Junior Olympic Team."

"God, that is so great!" Angie said, hugging Magdalena hard.

"But there is just one thing I want you to do, Angelina."

"Anything. What is it?"

"You've heard about the birth control pill?"

"Well, yeah, a few of us girls are taking them at the barn."

Magdalena held a French fry midair. "Really?"

"Don't look so surprised. You aren't my mother for everything. Why do you ask?"

"Well, since you are sexually active, I wanted you to see a doc and get a prescription."

"I already have. All of us at the barn see this doc that gives us a prescription."

Amazed at Angie's answers, all Magdalena could think of to say was, "And you follow the regimen for them to be effective."

"No, we feed them to the horses! Geez, Em, have a little faith. Whatever you say, I'll do, Em. I just want to go to Hawaii."

Magdalena released a long sigh while looking at her sister. *Mama was right - Angie is a ribelle.*

*****

Following Magdalena's failed date with Lance, she carefully avoided him. She never wanted to see him again socially. Accepting a date with him had been a foolish mistake. She held no malice for him; he was just irrelevant to her. One good thing that had come from that debacle was seeing the gynecologist. Her first sexual experience would be as she wished. Now, no man would believe he had made her his conquest.

Another positive was that she did see a marked improvement in her father's mobility under Lance's care. Del now used the stair rail with one hand and cane with the other to ascend the staircase. His left foot still slapped the floor when he walked, but he left the wheelchair behind more and more. His speech was another matter. Magdalena had stretched the use of appearance lawyers for court about as far as she could without jeopardizing clients and alarming Sciacca. So when she hired Michael Tynan, she felt a sense of relief. Tynan could handle trial work until she passed the bar.

Tynan presented well, although she would advise him to see a proper tailor. His lanky frame held his suits like a coat rack. If anyone needed custom tailoring, he did. With a strong voice, and an honest convincing way, he would be good for criminal law. She might also advise him to grow his hair a bit longer. His crew cut reminded her of a marine.

Chapter 19

Early the next morning, Magdalena settled herself at the kitchen table before leaving for classes. "Good morning, Maria," she said absently while waiting for her daily espresso. Outwardly, Magdalena offered a cool side and today was no exception.

"Good morning *Signorina*," Maria said setting the old *Bialetti* coffeemaker on the stove and turning on the gas.

When the pot finished sputtering and her espresso served, Magdalena dipped her *biscotto* into the black liquid. "Maria, a man named Michael Tynan will arrive at 9 a.m. today. Let him in and show him into the office. He will be working for us Monday through Friday. Please serve him lunch in Papa's patio daily. Today, I will be back from classes before he leaves."

"*Si, Signorina*," Maria said. Magdalena downed her espresso and headed for her car.

After Magdalena drove off, Rosella entered the back door of the kitchen for her early cup of coffee with Maria, their time for morning gossip. "So, what is new with the D'Alessandro family," Rosella said, taking *biscotti* from the tin.

Maria's lips pursed in anger as she poured coffee for the two of them. "The *Signorina* is in charge of all. She runs the house, her father's life, and now, Angelina says she is going to arrange a trip for her to go to Hawaii."

"Really, you hear things in the kitchen I never hear, but don't you think Angelina is too young to go so far?" said Rosella.

With narrowed eyes, Maria nodded. "And Angelina is too *tempestosa*, how do you say? Wild," Maria said, setting her cup down hard.

*****

Before Angie left for Hawaii, she would compete in the National Amateur Horse Show at the Earl Warren show grounds in Santa Barbara. It was the largest junior horse show in the US. But this would be her last. At nineteen, a rider was no longer eligible for competition. In the preceding years of showing, Angie's prowess had become well known. Competitors always moaned when they saw her name in the program. With her winning history, expensive mounts and top-paid trainer, riding against her was daunting. Angelina D'Alessandro would leave behind an award-winning past in the junior riding world.

*****

Magdalena slowly walked with her father to the barn area where Angie's horses were stalled. The effort her father was making to attend this last show of Angie's concerned her. He was trying to prove he could do some distance walking and this was one of those times. "Over here Papa, I think that is American Royalty coming out of the horse trailer. His nickname is Chocolate Chip. He's pretty with his white blaze and chestnut color, isn't he, Papa?" She watched her father nod as he looked up at the large horse.

"He looks big. And Angie rides him?"

"Oh yes, and the next one too. But most of Angie's blue

ribbons were won riding this horse. He's a nice, calm horse."

Then Immigrant Song, Angie's jumper appeared, pawing at the trailer door. D'Alessandro stepped backwards, leery of the large jumper. With enlarged nostrils and roving eyes, the animal shook his thick black forelock aside, examining the new environment.

"I don't think I like this one."

"He's the expensive one, Papa. This is the one that is half American racehorse and half Hanovarian the German police breed. See how the photographers are all taking his picture?"

"I don't like him. Does Angelina have to ride him?"

"Yes, Papa. He is bred not to break down while jumping fences."

Angie came running to her father when she saw him looking at her jumper. After embracing her father, she said, "Isn't he beautiful, Daddy?"

Del was speechless when Wally, her trainer arrived. "Hello, Mr. D'Alessandro, I don't believe we have ever met," he said extending his hand. "Angie loves this stubborn horse, and I'm impressed with the way she can handle him. But I must tell you, Mr. D'Alessandro, he is amazingly talented. Sorry, I see other horses unloading, I must go."

Immigrant Song attempted to rear onto his hind legs. Del's eyes widened with apprehension at the display. "He's just spooked by a few things, Daddy, but I love him," Angie said, mesmerized by the animal. "Don't be afraid of him."

Magdalena saw her father's concern. "When I first saw Immigrant Song, Papa, his size and dark chocolate-colored coat, he reminded me of..." Magdalena stopped talking.

Her father was watching Angelina, face masked with

fear, knowing she was about to ride the huge creature.

"Does steam always rise from his body like that?" he asked Angelina.

Laughing, Angelina said, "Only when the air is cold, like today, Daddy. That's why Magdalena suggested his barn name should be Espresso."

*****

Through Sciacca, Magdalena had arranged for her and her father to be driven to Santa Barbara while Alberto drove the horse van. They went first to the Santa Barbara Biltmore to deposit their luggage. After they saw Angelina's horses, they took their seats in the viewing stands. Bundled against the damp cold of the Santa Barbara autumn, Magdalena hugged her father. "This will be Angie's last competition as a junior rider, Papa. Next, we will probably see her compete for the Junior Olympics in a foreign country, representing the US."

Being near the horses alarmed him. Magdalena could tell he dreaded them.

She felt her father was trying to muster some assurance when he said, "I guess this is not such a bad outcome for a girl who wouldn't study but gets an invitation to join the Junior Olympic Team. I am so proud of her."

Magdalena wished her father would occasionally mention that he was proud she would be sitting for the bar soon, but she knew Angie accomplishments took precedence and probably always would. She was pleased to hear how well her father formed his words since she'd hired a new speech therapist. And when he watched Angie ride, although he worried for her safety, he seemed happy, a rare emotion for him.

Magdalena arranged her scarf around her neck then turned to look in the stands behind her. All day she had felt someone's eyes were on her. No one stood out, yet she felt a presence spying on her the entire weekend. Her stomach, always a barometer of her anxiety, felt taut. She left her seat to get hot coffee for herself and her father. At the bottom of the steps, she turned to look up into the grandstands again and was surprised to see a Cozza brother seated high up against the wall. *What was he doing here?*

When she returned to her seat, Magdalena handed her father his coffee then sat close and ran her hand through his. She looked into his face. His furry eyebrows were now white, and his face was set with deep lines. He looked like a man in his seventies, not his sixties. His stroke had left a heavy mark on him. She sensed his anxiety. "What is bothering you, Papa?"

"Do you think Angie is ready for Hawaii, Magdalena?"

Diverted from her thoughts of being watched, she turned toward her father.

"Yes, Papa. The two chaperoning families are responsible people, and Angie will be well supervised. I have met with the girls and the parents."

Magdalena turned to glance behind her again. Had she imagined the Cozza brother? Were the brothers there protecting her against something? It was most unusual that they would travel to Santa Barbara to see Angie compete. She needed to talk to them. *No, I'll call Sciacca for an answer.* She decided.

The cold air brought chill but no rain to the show grounds offering good riding weather. Trainers milled about, giving last minute instructions to their young riders. Outside the horse ring, a schematic posted on a wall defined the course, its jumps, walls and fences. Angie never had to look at a diagram more than once or twice to grasp its path.

Today the riders had to maneuver through the ring twice, ride the course as outlined and take nine fences, clean.

Across the large ring, a loud speaker announced: "Angelia D'Alessandro, riding Immigrant Song." Entering the ring, she looked like she was riding a giant rocking horse. Her still, gloved hands guided her eager mount to the first fence. Immigrant Song took it with ease, legs tucked high against his chest. With a smooth and rhythmic cadence, Angie and her jumper took each obstacle with skill and confidence. The sounds from the crowd swelled with each fence they took clean. The water jump stopped many horses. Immigrant Song made the long leap across the water effortlessly. Angie turned and headed for the last barrier: a colorful gate built like a picket fence. Spectators were at the rail, several with cameras. The camera flashes were noisy and too many. This mighty horse, frightened by the lights, abruptly planted his hooves before the gate. His halt sent Angie flying over the fence to the ground, where she lay in the dirt, motionless. The horse tried desperately to complete his task. Without a rider to guide him, his effort was clumsy. His leap headed him toward Angie who lay sprawled on the ground. By twisting his trunk in midair, like a giant snake, he avoided landing on top of her. This gyration plunged him to the ground upside down. The barrel of his body hit the earth with the sound of a loud drumbeat. His fall missed Angelina by a hand. The crowd stood in horror. The horse's grunts and writhing showed his pain. Angie lay still next to him.

"Oh no, not my Angelina!" Del said, struggling to rise. Trying again, he steadied himself on the back rail of his seat, his body swaying. Magdalena helped him regain his balance and slowly they descended the grandstands. It was a short walk to the tented infirmary where Angie had been taken. Her father's labored steps and heavy breathing made the walk slow. Being out of the wheelchair was beginning to take its toll. His skin had turned gray.

"Papa the ambulance is still at the tent. That's a good sign," Magdalena said, noticing how tired he had become. When they entered the tent, Angie was sipping a cup of water and flirting with the medic.

The medic stood. "She was simply knocked out cold, Sir," he said, standing. Then looking at D'Alessandro he added, "Sir, you don't look too well. Please have a seat." Under the lights of the pavilion, Magdalena could see clearly her father's ashen pallor.

When the medic pulled the BP cuff from her father's arm, the reading was 200 over 120, prompting the young man to advise Del to see his doctor as soon as possible.

"What's wrong with Daddy, Em?" Angie asked

"Angie, are you okay?" called her trainer, poking his head into the tent entrance.

"Yeah, I'm good, Wally. How is Espresso?"

"Not as good as you look. I'll get back to you later," he said.

Magdalena shook her head. Horses, that's all Wally and Angie really care about, she thought.

The medic looked seriously at Magdalena. "There's a golf cart outside, Miss. I'll reserve it for you and your father's use," he discreetly whispered into Magdalena's ear. Don't forget. Your father should visit his doctor as soon as he returns to L.A."

Chapter 20

Once back in their hotel suite, Magdalena quietly closed the door to her father's bedroom. With Angie's last event over, she hoped her father would be amenable to leave for home soon. Magdalena didn't want him to trek back to the show grounds for Angie's award ceremony for best in show. He had seen most of her wins that led to her receiving the grand championship. Magdalena knew that when Angie brought home her trophy, that would be enough for him. His exhaustion concerned Magdalena, so she decided to let him rest. She sat down to call Sciacca.

When Del picked up the phone to order a pot of coffee, Magdalena's dialing sound clicked in his ear. He was about to hang up the receiver, but the fear that Angie's injury was more serious led him to listen to Magdalena's call. What came next overtook Del with a shock from which he would never fully recover.

Magdalena spoke softly with friendliness and respect. "Hello, Mr. Sciacca, it's Magdalena."

"Hello, Magdalena. I think I must begin calling you my goddaughter?"

Del's face turned dark and motionless. As he drew short breaths, knots formed at his jaw. Along with clammy skin, all the signs were there of his escalating blood pressure. Holding the phone close, Del's hand covered the mouthpiece tight.

Magdalena's cheerful tone came across the line. "I'm fine, and thank you for calling me goddaughter. May I speak to you about something?"

"Shoot, you know I'm always at your disposal, Magdalena," said Sciacca.

"Well, we, or rather I, hired a new lawyer for our team. His name is Michael Tynan. Papa still isn't quite up to representing clients in court yet, so I have been trying to think ahead. This man is exceedingly qualified with a resume much like mine. I have him working on briefs as we speak."

Sciacca voice carried a modicum of suspicion about the hire.

Del's eyes narrowed when he heard that Tynan had full rein of his office files.

"Go on Magdalena," Sciacca said in a more serious tone.

"As you know, I wanted to sit second chair to my father after passing the bar."

"Yes, I recall you saying that. Go on with what you wanted to tell me."

"What I believe will happen next is that I'll sit second chair to Tynan, not Papa. A short time after that, I will move to take over the practice.

"You *are* thinking ahead, Magdalena, and I agree in general with what you propose. I appreciate you calling and telling me about your father. Is he really that unable to handle cases anymore?"

"I think his best days are behind him, Mr. Sciacca."

As Del continued to listen, his breaths grew shorter and his dry mouth wouldn't allow him to swallow.

"All right, assuming that is true, I need something from you as soon as possible," Sciacca said.

"Yes, Mr. Sciacca, what would that be?"

"I want the address and phone number of this Tynan you have hired."

"Of course, I'll do that the moment we return home. I'm sure we will be back today."

Magdalena slowly hung up the receiver, stared pensively into space. Could there be something about Michael Tynan she didn't know? And she forgot entirely to mention that she felt she was being watched, or even to ask why one or both of the Cozza brothers might be in Santa Barbara.

Magdalena's conversation with Sciacca left Dominic D'Alessandro with a stab to his heart that he carried with him forever.

He needed a drink. He slipped out of their suite while Magdalena was in her shower. His head pounded as he navigated his way to the downstairs bar. Finding a dark corner in the cocktail lounge, Del signaled a waiter "A double Brandy, and can you plug in a telephone here."

The waiter nodded and promptly returned with both.

After downing his drink, Del dialed the phone set before him. While waiting for the other end, he whispered to himself, "Magdalena has embraced the gangsters."

Someone answered. Del cleared his throat. "Hello Harold, I have a job for you."

"Anything you say, Mr. D," said Del's P.I.

"I want you to check on a guy named Tynan. Michael Tynan?"

"What are we looking for Mr. D?"

"I think he might be FBI, I want you to find out."

"Whoa, one of the spooks, huh."

"Maybe. Just find out all about him."

"You got it, Mr. D. Any special place I can find him?"

"Yeah, at my house 9 a.m. to 5 p.m."

"No shit, Sir?"

"No shit, Harold, and this can't be done fast enough."

"I'm on it," Harold answered.

As Del raised an empty glass toward the waiter, his headache begun to abate.

*****

Magdalena asked Alberto to drive her and her father home due to his poor health. and told Angie to have Wally drive the horse trailer back to the barn in Pacific Palisades

Her father's silence during the trip bothered Magdalena. She wanted to get him to his doctor as soon as possible. "Papa, do you mind if I call your doctor from the car phone and make an appointment? Remember what the medic said about your blood pressure."

"No, never mind." her father flatly answered.

Turning away from her, he had nothing more to say. Now she knew something else was amiss. During the two-hour drive her father's eyes were closed, but Magdalena suspected that he was feigning sleep. *What has provoked papa to be so distant? Was he resigned to his illness?* Deep down she didn't feel his illness explained his mood.

*****

Once back home, Angie talked about Hawaii and counted the days until she would fly there. It couldn't happen fast enough for her. When the actual day to depart arrived, she badgered Magdalena about leaving. "When do we leave for the airport, Em?"

"I told you five minutes ago, Angie, we leave in two hours."

"Jeez, that long? Can't we leave earlier?"

"No, Angie," Magdalena answered firmly. "Why don't you go and speak to Papa, and at least thank him for allowing you this trip. He's going to miss you a lot."

"Okay," Angie said in a huff.

Outside his office, Del sat on his patio behind the French doors. Inside, Michael Tynan worked on briefs that Magdalena had assigned him.

"Daddy, there you are," Angie said, kissing him on the cheek and pulling a patio chair next to him.

"Hello, my little *Championessa.* You all ready for Hawaii?"

"I'm ready, but Magdalena won't leave early. Daddy, are you okay? You look sad."

"I'm all right, I just have to slow down until my blood pressure is under control."

"Magdalena said you are going to get some new medicine from your doctor."

"Yes, I am, and I think it will help. I'm glad you're here, Angelina. I want to talk to you. Shut the doors to the office." He scooted his chair closer to her. "Angie, can you keep a secret?"

She complied and sat closer, too. "If *you* tell it to me, I can, Daddy."

"Okay, this is the secret, and it is important that you don't tell Magdalena."

Angie's head rose, with a serious face, trying to look more important than her sister.

A sober tone marked Del's words. "If anything happens to me, I want you to see Gino. He has a box under his bed for you. It's filled with cash."

Angie eyes welled. "Daddy, you sound like you're maybe: planning to die."

"No, but if I do, you go to Gino. Promise me?"

Angie bit at her lip, her head nodding slowly. "Is there a box for Magdalena too?"

Del shook his head. "No, Angelina. Your sister will run the law practice when I am gone and make her own money."

Del failed to say that originally, he had planned that the cash under Gino's bed be shared between his daughters.

"How did you get the money, Daddy?"

"It's a long story, my *bionda*. I may tell you some day. Now go, have a wonderful time in Hawaii."

*****

After Angelina had left for Hawaii, Del remained on the patio through the early evening, and began to reminisce just how he did get the money that Gino was hiding. It was all too easy, he remembered.

It had started with a court decision that became a law when he was a D.A. in San Francisco. Little did he think he would one day use that law against his own clients in L.A., and to his benefit. But, beginning in the 1970's, that's exactly what D'Alessandro did.

For more than a decade, he masterfully extorted a hoard of cash from the gangsters he represented in excess of $500,000. Sitting very still in his office patio, he whispered to himself the words of the court in 1966:

The fifth Amendment privilege against self-incrimination requires law enforcement officials advise a suspect interrogated in custody of his or her rights to remain silent and to obtain an attorney...

Most cops and criminals, and even lawyers, were slow to understand or use what was called the Miranda Law. As soon as he became a counselor for the Mafia, Del used the new law to extort money from the gangsters he viewed with contempt. When a gang members was arrested, he was to contact D'Alessandro. Del's first move was to covertly determine if the arrested man, had been read his Miranda Rights. Early on, most police officers failed to do this which allowed Del to get anybody off in a minute.

D'Alessandro would tell ignorant gangsters, that he needed money to pay off somebody to get them released. They would sweat awhile if they didn't have the money on hand, but in the end, they always came up with what they thought was payoff money. This was a way of life for gangsters; The Mafia operated largely by demanding bribes.

After receiving the money, D'Alessandro would get the suspect released.

The arrestees never questioned his demands. It had been easy to beat them at their own game. Until the police learned to read Miranda Rights, every time a suspect was held, D'Alessandro squeezed tens of thousands of dollars from those arrested, on top of his big salary as counselor. There were times when he speculated if it was in his blood to do this. He had suffered as a kid being called a wop, a Guinea and mobster. Those slurs had remained with him. Early in his career in San Francisco, he had quietly changed his family name from Mancuso, a common Mafia surname in Palermo. Although he had no connection with these hoodlums, he always hated any reference to Palermo, the birthplace of the Mafia.

Chapter 21

After two weeks in Hawaii, the parents who were chaperoning the girls called from the Royal Hawaiian Hotel to express worry over Angie's remote behavior. They said they were concerned that she wasn't participating in excursions with the other girls. As a result, the chaperons couldn't keep track of her.

Over the years, Magdalena had never heard Angie's behavior described as remote. Angie could be called impetuous and hotheaded and always up front about her activities. What could she be up to?

A second call from the parents stated that Angie had flown to the island of Molokai. They were beside themselves with worry, and implored Magdalena to take over responsibility for Angie during the last two weeks of their vacation. In fact, they were adamant that they took no further responsibility for her actions.

Angry, Magdalena knew she had to locate her sister. *Damn Angelina Why is she acting so recklessly?* It took little time on the telephone for Magdalena to track her to the only good hotel on the island, the Sheraton Molokai.

Magdalena was livid, as she waited for Angie to pick up the lobby phone.

"Angie, what *are* you doing in Molokai?" Not waiting

for an answer, Magdalena continued shouting. "You've worried everyone! Come home immediately!"

"I'm having a great time. I've met someone, and I'm staying here."

Magdalena collected herself. "You have met someone? What exactly does that mean, Angie?"

"It means I have met a man I love, and I am going to stay here and live with him."

"Angie, this will kill Papa. You must come home so we can sit down and talk."

"I'll talk to Daddy on my own. I've decided not to join the Olympic team, so I can stay here. Besides, you're going to take over the business anyway, so don't worry about me."

"Wait a minute. Where did you hear that I was going to take over the business?"

"Daddy told me. I have to go." The phone went to dial tone.

Magdalena collapsed in a chair with the receiver in her lap, until she heard the Hawaiian operator ask her to release the line. From Angie's comment about Magdalena taking over the business, she deduced that her father must have listened in on her conversation with Sciacca. That explained his cold behavior toward her on the way home from Santa Barbara, and ever since. For a moment, she wished her sister dead.

What should she do next? Try and have a talk with her father about the future of the law practice? Cut Angie's American Express credit off? Or tell her father what Angie had just announced? Magdalena's mind whirled. Knowing that Papa favored Angie made the decision all the more difficult.

She had a plan, a sound strategy to run the practice. Having been exposed to her father's workload and assisting him regularly, he should understand her capabilities and her motivation to help. It wasn't supposed to happen this way.

But deep in her soul, Magdalena knew she could do little to appease her father, let alone gain his recognition. She resented Angelina for all the attention and love she got from Del. She rushed to her bathroom and heaved until her throat felt raw and sore.

Looking into her bathroom mirror, she went over her face with a cool washcloth and made a decision. For a time, she would ignore Angie's crazy declaration to live with this man in Molokai. What a bitch Angie was turning out to be. Magdalena didn't even know who this guy was. She admonished herself for having gotten so angry with her sister and to learn so little. It wasn't often she lost control as she had done on the phone with Angie. She should have remained calm and learned more.

And something about Angie's tone bothered Magdalena. There was a detachment in her voice, a distance she hadn't heard before.

By the fourth week of Angie's trip away, Magdalena still hadn't decided on a tactic to open a dialogue with her father. Then Sunday evening, as she walked by his office, he called to her. "Magdalena, isn't this the week Angie comes home?"

Magdalena walked into his sanctuary, noting that he had reorganized his desk. She hesitantly sat in a chair across from him. Through the French doors, the setting sun beamed a warm glow over the room. "It's a lovely evening isn't it Papa?" Magdalena said carefully.

Del did not acknowledge her comment, or look up from his desk. "I asked about Angie."

How angry he sounded! Magdalena sighed. "I think she is staying a few extra days, I will be talking to her tonight,"

Magdalena lied. "Papa, are you all right?"

With a sour look on his face, he glared at her. "I am much better than you and Sciacca think I am. I will be going back to work in this office tomorrow, and you will be terminating Michael Tynan. You hired an FBI agent, Magdalena. And of course, you'll be the one to tell your godfather about that fuck up."

Stunned, Magdalena sat rigid. She started to apologize. But when her father held up a hand, she immediately stood and silently walked out of his office.

That night, she learned that the chaperones, responsible for the six girls had returned home with five. Magdalena queried them at length but learned nothing more of Angie and her mystery man in Molokai.

After her conversation with the parents, she knew she had to tell Papa about Angie. Then she had to deal with the Tynan issue, and also apologize to Sciacca for hiring an FBI agent. She thought it best not to reveal to Sciacca that her father had listened in on their conversation in Santa Barbara. Her trip to the bathroom to relieve herself of the build-up of bile did little to clear her guilt. She felt trapped, like a spider caught in its own web.

Before doing anything else, she decided to do a little investigating of her own. No doubt her father had used his long-time investigator, Harold, to learn Tynan's identity. Sciacca had likely done the same. Now it was her turn. She checked her dictionary where she hid private bits of information. Under the letter 'C,' she found the scrap of paper Joey Cozza had once handed her. "Call me anytime you need help," he had said. She called and asked Joey to meet her at the Bel Air Hotel the next day for lunch.

Chapter 22

Cruising down Stone Canyon to the Bel Air, Magdalena turned her Jaguar behind large hedges to stop at valet parking. A young attendant opened her car door with a flourish, his expression revealing how much he admired her white halter-top and maroon bell-bottoms. “Welcome, Miss D’Alessandro.”

The warm day brought streaks of glittering sunlight to the lake as Magdalena paused on the bridge to watch a pair of swans preening one another. She remembered reading that they mated for life. For a moment, she considered the sad thought that she would never mate for life.

She crossed the bridge. The lush containers of gardenias, ferns and orchids marked her path to the garden room. She glided confidently into the restaurant with not a trace of her limp, her corrective shoes concealed by her bell-bottom slacks. The hotel maître d’ politely addressed her as Miss D’Alessandro and escorted her to the corner table she had reserved.

Magdalena was unprepared for the debonair man who stood holding a chair for her. With no trace of his former mobster look, Joey Cozza had matured into a confident man. He wore a beautifully tailored suit, and Magdalena was not the only woman in the restaurant to notice him. *He turns heads like a beautiful woman,* she observed.

With an attentive demeanor, he stood offering her his hand. "*Buona sera,* Magdalena," he said with the quiet aplomb of a refined gentleman.

"*Buona sera,* Joseph." She could no longer call him Joey. "I'm glad you could meet me so soon.

Joseph Cozza nodded, as if to say I will always be ready to meet you.

Magdalena thought this would be an easy meeting, she would tell him what she wanted investigated and that would be that. But Joseph was making it difficult, with his piercing gaze that showed he admired and wanted her.

"We haven't seen you at the house lately, Joseph," Magdalena said as she tried to ignore the warm spell he had cast upon her. But she welcomed his gentility and attention. Little of her life held either. This meeting felt good in contrast to the difficulties at home with her father, the trouble Angie was causing not to mention having hired an FBI agent.

Nodding in answer, Joseph sat observing her from across the table with continuing interest. "You haven't seen me because I was in Italy for several months when my mother died."

Magdalena sighed. "I am very sorry to hear about your mother, Joseph."

"She had been ill a long time," he said, turning away. "It was expected."

The conversation about the death of his mother did nothing to eclipse the mutual glow that enveloped them. Joseph's attention struck her like looking into the sun. She felt blinded in this unfamiliar territory realizing their feelings were shared.

Both sat in silence for a time as she reminded herself

why she had asked Cozza to join her for lunch, and discuss the assignment she had for him.

"May I take your cocktail order before lunch?" The waiter said, interrupting their mood.

Joseph deferred to Magdalena, who said, "I'll have a champagne cocktail."

"A dry martini for me," Joseph said.

"My father drinks an occasional martini, but prefers brandy," was all Magdalena could think of to say, still inhibited by the magnetism that persisted between them.

"And how is your father recovering from his stroke?"

"How did you know my father had a stroke?"

"Vinnie has kept me in touch."

She looked at Joseph with a new curiosity, as something dawned on her. "It was Vinnie in Santa Barbara watching Papa and me, wasn't it? Or was it both of you?"

Readjusting the napkin in his lap, Joseph said nothing.

Uneasy, Magdalena asked, "Why have you had someone watching me, Joseph?"

"It's not watching, Magdalena, it's protection."

"And I suppose that comes from Sciacca?" Magdalena asked.

"No, it comes from me."

Confounded by such stealth, Magdalena hoped she wouldn't have to make a trip to the restroom. It would be too much to learn that she made another miscalculation in judging people.

"How long has this been going on, Joseph?"

She saw affection mixed with loyalty in his expression as he responded.

"Ever since you were fourteen and put in the hospital by that animal, Cavallaro."

Magdalena sat back in her chair, amazed that she had

been under Cozza's protection for nearly ten years. "Did you literally have me followed everywhere, Joseph?"

"No. It was more like checking up on you weekly, or if you went away for a few days, like the horse show in Santa Barbara." After their cocktails arrived Joseph attempted to change the subject. "How *is* your sister?"

Magdalena took a generous drink of her cocktail, relieved that Joseph had broached the subject of Angie. She could now open the conversation about her sister with some control. "Angie went to Hawaii with her equestrian friends and now she won't come home." Magdalena couldn't reveal to Joseph that Angie wanted to stay there to live with a man she said she loved. Magdalena always held things back.

"What can I do?"

"Actually, Joseph, I think I have to go there and talk some sense to her."

"I will go with you."

Not liking where this was going, she altered her tack. "I'm still trying to formulate my plans. My father always favored Angie, but I am the one stuck watching out for her.'

"Yeah, I got stuck with my brother too."

Magdalena smiled.

A second order of drinks arrived.

"Here's to getting your sister home," Joseph said softly.

Chapter 23

As Rosella vacuumed, she passed the ringing phone in the entry alcove. Del was back at work in his office, and never took house line calls. Rosella didn't like answering the phone, but finally shut off the vacuum and reached into the niche for the receiver.

"Hello, D'Alessandro residence," Rosella answered with apprehension. Due to a poor connection, the housekeeper found it difficult hearing the person on the other end of the line. From the top of the staircase, Magdalena called, "Ask who it is Rosella."

Rosella couldn't understand the name of the caller and held the receiver up high towards Magdalena, shaking her head.

Magdalena hurried down the stairs. "Hello," she said. "Yes, this is the D'Alessandro residence, but I can barely hear you. Could you please speak up?"

Rosella had returned to her vacuuming. Magdalena waved at her to turn off the machine after realizing she was speaking with the Waikiki police department.

"Please talk louder," she said. "That's better, yes my sister is Angelina D'Alessandro."

The next words that followed caused Magdalena to collapse beside the alcove. Painfully, she asked, "Could you please repeat that? I don't think I heard you correctly." When the police officer's words were repeated, Magdalena let the receiver tumble to her floor. She stared into the silence, hearing again the Waikiki police officer confirm Angie's death.

*****

Churning inside, Magdalena softly knocked on her father's office door. Since her conversation with Sciacca, Del had showed dislike for her that bordered on hatred. And now she had to deliver the worst news possible.

"Yes," called her father gruffly.

She walked into his office and stood silent for a moment. "Papa, I have terrible news."

"I thought I had already heard your worst news, Magdalena," his voice full of sarcasm.

She knew he referred to the alliance she had formed with Sciacca. Magdalena took a big breath, sighed then spoke with care, forcing her lips to say the words. "Papa it's about Angie."

He looked up from his paperwork. "Angie, what about Angie?"

Magdalena swallowed and licked her lips.

"I just talked to the Waikiki Police Department. Angie has been found dead. Her body washed up on the beach in Molokai last night." Magdalena tightened her grip on the paper she held behind her with the number of the Hawaiian police department. She watched her father's jaw slacken and the pen drop from his hand.

"What did you say?"

"Angie has been found dead, Papa."

The gruffness in him disappeared, replaced by disbelief. Sitting erect, streaks of anger crossed his face like lightning. "Where did you hear this?"

Immediately, she could see his animosity mounting, clearly wanting to place blame on her.

Magdalena stood silently.

"Answer me, give me some answers!" he bellowed.

Magdalena shook her head but said nothing more.

"Get me the number of the police, and get out of my sight," he growled, overriding his shock with anger.

Magdalena slapped down the phone number. "Papa, are you sure I can't make the call for you?"

The look he threw at her was charged with rancor as he waved her away. She stepped outside his office and closed the door to listen. His voice was muffled, and she couldn't hear well through the door. But she could tell that he verified that Angie was dead. Then came his expected words.

"No, not my Angelina, my *amore,* my *bionda,*" he slurred.

Once again, Papa's favoritism for Angie hit Magdalena. How many times over the years had she heard him say that Angelina, like Mama, was the fairer one?

She heard her father cry out and the phone receiver drop to the floor. Then came the sound of his desk chair overturning with a loud thump.

*****

Minutes later, an ambulance took her father to the Santa Monica hospital with Magdalena sitting near him in the wailing vehicle. The attendants had no time to speak with her as they busied over her father. The vehicle sped to the emergency entrance of the hospital, and made a quick stop. Attendants whisked her father's gurney through doors where she was refused entry.

*****

Once in the hospital reception area, Magdalena paced

the room, distraught about what her father's diagnosis would be. This time she was without Angie.

It wasn't long before a rotund man approached her. Speaking proper English with a Spanish accent and a caring manner, he stood before her. "Miss D'Alessandro, I presume?"

Magdalena nodded," expecting the worst.

"I'm Dr. Peña. We believe your father has suffered a stroke but we will know more tomorrow. We are glad you got him here quickly. That can sometimes make a big difference." Magdalena nodded wondering what the outcome of a second stroke would be.

"Will he live, Doctor?"

The doctor held both her hands. "Yes, I believe he probably will. Now I suggest you go home. There is nothing more you can do here tonight. We can talk tomorrow."

Magdalena looked away, not wanting to show a stranger her tears.

"Do you have someone who can drive you home?" Doctor Peña asked.

Magdalena nodded without thinking.

After the doctor left, she realized she had no way home and had been responding like a robot. Coming to her senses, she called Joseph.

*****

Joseph found Magdalena sitting alone in a far corner of the waiting room. She looked like a child lost in some kind of daydream. Quietly he sat next to her and put his arm around her. "What can I do Magdalena?"

She looked at him as though he was a stranger. In a few words, she told him her father had another stroke. She said it was her fault for telling him that Angelina was found dead in Molokai. Joseph showed no emotion and asked no questions. He guided her to his car and drove her home in silence.

*****

Joseph's El Dorado made a crunching sound as it came to a gradual stop on the pebbles of the car court.

Alberto ran down the stairs from the garage apartment and asked, "Mr. D? Is he…"

"He is alive," Joseph said. Before Alberto retreated to his apartment, Joseph drew him near with a forefinger to whisper to him that Angelina was dead.

Joseph took Magdalena's hand. "I think you could use a drink."

Magdalena's nod was mechanical. She headed for her father's office where the liquor was stored. Joseph followed her and, once inside, righted her father's chair. He looked up to see Magdalena dumbstruck, holding a cut-glass decanter in one hand and a glass in the other.

"I'll take that," Joseph said, moving quickly to remove the liquor and glass from her shaking hands. "You sit down." He guided her to the couch.

Joseph poured her a Brandy. "Drink up," he said, firmly placing the glass in her hand.

She drank, and asked for another, and another.

"That's enough, Magdalena."

"I don't feel like I've have had any alcohol at all. Why is that?"

"Sometimes that happens when you're full of adrenalin; it's hard to come down."

Magdalena tried to stand and wavered. Joseph reached to steady her. He was surprised when she took hold of his tie and pulled him close. Looking into her face, Joseph saw that her black eyes were wells of pain. *How did her sister die?* Lifting her lips to his, he was surprised by her languid kiss. The touch of her lips conveyed much to Joseph. He thought he could feel her exhaustion from enduring her father's stroke, and maybe, even relief in her sister's passing.

Her passion, both sad and intense, made Joseph reel. "I've never been kissed like that before, Magdalena," he said, holding her close. Now her sobs began, they were raw and unrestrained. Her checks streamed with tears of release, the liquor beginning to take its effect. Joseph could feel the front of his shirt dampen from her crying.

When she seemed finished with her outpouring, he allowed her to take his hand and unceremoniously lead him from her father's office, up the staircase to her bedroom.

Joseph slowly began to undress her. She stood there in a mental fog. He could see disrobing her didn't excite Magdalena. For Joseph, it couldn't have been more sensual. As he looked into her questioning eyes, then at her beautiful body, he realized that Magdalena knew little about having sex. "Magdalena, is this your first time?"

Joseph said as he watched the liquor continue to take its affect.

"How can you tell?" she answered with a thick tongue.

He held her close and smiled. "I'll tell you someday, but now let's get you in bed. "I think you are about to pass out."

Joseph found himself in a new situation. His early sex life found him pursuing a number of women, many whom he had lured into bed. Tonight, Magdalena coaxed him to hers. It made Joseph happy to be with the woman he had loved since she was a child, yet something told him their lovemaking did not have a future.

He laid the covers over her as she was losing consciousness. He shed his clothes and couldn't resist crawling in next to her, slipping under the covers to hold her in his arms.

The hours moved slowly for Joseph, who had always wanted to make love to Magdalena. His mind churned and his body ached, as sleep eluded him. The pain in his groin had just begun to wane, when before dawn, he received two surprises. One came from an opened drape revealing the brightness of the full moon. The other came from Magdalena. Joseph felt her turn and face him. The glow from the moonbeams bathed her striking nakedness. Her languid kissing began again. Then, not only did she make exquisite love with him, but the luminous moon made the experience visual and unforgettable for Joseph. He reveled in her body. And as the beams illuminated their lovemaking, Magdalena showered her pent sexuality upon him.

Joseph woke to the sound of Magdalena showering. Lying in bed waiting for her, his thoughts screamed, *Jesus, how could this have been her first time to make, love?*

Chapter 24

Of the seven days Magdalena's father remained in the hospital, she visited him morning and evening. "Good morning Papa. How are you feeling today?" Her father made no effort to respond. She assumed that this stroke was more severe than the last and hoped his remoteness was the result of it. "Gino sends you flowers from the yard, Papa. He says you must get well to see the hydrangeas blooming, and that he has more bell peppers than Maria can preserve in jars." Her father offered no response, to her words. After conferring with his doctors, Magdalena learned that this stroke had severely impaired her father's ability to speak or use his left side, and that he would likely be confined to a wheel chair from now on, indefinitely. The doctors further agreed that physical therapy could commence again, but she should *not* expect the strides her father had made after his first stroke.

On the fifth day when Magdalena arrived to visit her father, she found him with a small blackboard at his side and a piece of chalk marked with illegible words. She leaned down to kiss his forehead. His skin was the color of gray flannel, his bushy eyebrows and his hair were now coming in white. The creases around his eyes were far more prominent. "More flowers from Gino, Papa," she said laying them on a table.

Magdalena reached for a chair and moved it close to his bed. She prayed that her words wouldn't anger him or trigger another stroke. To broach the subject of Angie, she wanted to be brief, yet clear. "Papa, Angie's casket will arrive on a flight tomorrow at LAX." She saw her father's right-hand ball into a fist, while his left stayed immobile. "I will be there to meet the plane, Papa. I found a local mortuary that can make arrangements to keep Angie until you decide on a date for her funeral. Is that what you would like, Papa?" Just half of her father's face worked, but both eyes teared up. She thought she saw his head nod.

Leaving the hospital, she was in deep thought as she walked through the exit with the large and silent automatic doors. The scrawl of words on her father's chalkboard, which no one at the hospital could decipher, stuck in her mind like a puzzle. The unfinished word had begun with "ele..."

*****

When Magdalena returned home from her hospital visits, Maria would relay messages from Joseph. "He calls to ask how you and your father are, *Senorina.* And look at the *grande,* large orchids he sends to the house," Maria said motioning toward a huge plant on the entry table. None of the staff mentioned Angelina's death.

Magdalena chose not to return Joseph's calls. Instead she immersed herself in books on criminal law from the shelves in her father's office. She could always go to a place in her brain that blocked out unwelcome reality. She formed this habit in high school when her father paid her little attention. She also found that the recordings of Rachmaninoff did the same. But when she played

Rachmaninoff's Piano Concerto Number 3 today, memories of Joseph came to mind. It was a scratchy recording from 1939, but Rachmaninoff himself played his composition on the piano.

She had begun to think about Joseph, and how easily they had sex. Everything they did in bed seemed so natural. It was truly amazing how lovemaking didn't have to be taught. She would be intimate again with Joseph, but when *she* chose. She would continue with her contraception pills. The thought brought a smile to her face. Like her father she could recall parts of the law, verbatim. The Supreme Court's 1965 decision was one of those recollections: Griswold v. Connecticut stating that it was unconstitutional for the government to prohibit married couples from using birth control… If there was a beginning to the sexual revolution, she thought, that was it. She knew she and Joseph would become intimate again, and that could lead to a proposal from him. Sciacca had intimated that Joseph wanted to marry her and she couldn't let that happen.

Her thoughts were interrupted by a call from the hospital. "Hello, Magdalena, this is Doctor Peña. Your father is ready to return home."

"Oh, I am so happy to hear that, Doctor. When can I pick him up?"

"Actually, your father is very specific about that. He wants a man named Alberto to come alone and drive him home."

"Of course, that is our chauffeur and Papa's aide. I'll tell him to come at once, and thank you for the call."

This latest rebuff from her father sent Magdalena back to Rachmaninoff.

*****

Later in the day, she heard the front door open and

Alberto push her father's wheelchair into the entry. Magdalena looked down on him from the landing, "Hello Papa, I'm so glad to see you home." She rushed down the stairs and immediately noticed the chalkboard on his lap. ELEVATOR - INSTALL, it read in large letters. Clearly her father's brain worked well enough to express his needs, just not to say them. When he made a feeble effort to point the board toward the staircase, it fell from his tenuous grip and shattered into pieces. Magdalena rushed to retrieve the shards. "Of course, Papa, I will find someone to install one as soon as possible." He did not acknowledge her.

At the sound of the blackboard hitting the floor, Romulus and Remus came running. As they romped toward their master they lost traction on the marble floor and slid up next to him. With long tongues and smiles on their ruffled lips they looked embarrassed. When Del ran his right hand over the huge heads of the dogs, the mastiffs responded with wiggling bodies and whimpers.

Watching the scene, Magdalena thought, *I wish Papa loves me just a fraction of the amount that he loves the dogs.*

*****

After leaving L.A. Airport, Magdalena followed the hearse to the funeral home. She had thought of asking Joseph to be part of this process, but in the end decided, to keep it a private matter. The mortuary had made storage arrangements for Angelina's body somewhere until the funeral could be planned. She really didn't want to know where. She hadn't realized that Angie's effects, as the Molokai Sheraton labeled them, would arrive with her body. A lot of paper signing was necessary both at the airport and the mortuary. Magdalena reflected that for a student of the law, she had read very little of what she had signed.

Once home, she quietly opened the door to her father's office intending to give him an abbreviated report of what she had just accomplished. She met Alberto tiptoeing out with a finger to his lips. Outside the office, Magdalena drew him aside. "Is Papa okay?"

"Yes, he has just fallen asleep on the couch with the dogs."

"Are you able to care for my father, or would you like me to call in someone from the medical profession?"

Alberto's face turned sad.

"No, I can do it - if you want to have someone come to help with his exercises and speech, that is good. But I can do it."

"You're sure?" she asked.

"I am sure, *Senorina*."

"You must promise me that if you find it too difficult, you will tell me and I will call in someone to help you."

"Yes, *Senorina*, I will tell you if that happens," he assured her.

She hoped Alberto would volunteer on more than he could handle. Her mind returned to how Alberto had taken on the man who had attacked her with a tire iron. Yes, she decided, *Alberto can handle his job*.

Upstairs, she trudged to her bedroom, happy for small things. She had found headphones for the plug on her Califone record player. Now she could listen without disturbing papa.

Chapter 25

First Papa wanted to have Angelina's body flown to San Francisco and lay her to rest next to Mama. Then he changed his mind. Her father showed less patience communicating after this second stroke. He angrily pecked on the keys of his IBM Selectric, 'Angelina in crypt.'

She wondered if he would ever speak again. His right hand went on to type short phrases about a little cemetery in Westwood that housed a mausoleum where famous people were interred. He typed that he wanted this to be his *championessa's* resting place. Magdalena figured that Harold, her father's investigator, had aided him in locating the cemetery. Papa certainly had not been relying on her.

I guess it will be Potter's Field for me. But maybe after Papa gets used to Angie being gone, he will love me a little more.

Not having to make funeral arrangements was a relief for Magdalena and, knowing the precision Harold applied to his work, he would undoubtedly do a good job for Papa.

It had been a macabre experience, waiting for the autopsy, organizing a transport from Oahu to L.A. and finding a mortuary to hold the body until a funeral could be arranged. All that had been quite enough for Magdalena. *Angie could wreak havoc, even after her death. How typical of her.* Sighing, Magdalena remembered that Angie's suitcases were still in her car. She tracked down Alberto and had him lug the cases upstairs to Angie's bedroom.

After unpacking the contents, Magdalena bagged most of the items to send off to a charitable organization. The job had exhausted her, not the unpacking, but the ongoing dealings with Angie's detritus. Emotionally drained, she wondered if a message lay behind all of this? Could any of Angie's items say something about her mysterious death? There had been no word from the Hawaii Police Department. She was sitting on her sister's bed, staring into space, when she remembered all the equestrian gear yet to sort through, not to mention Angie's horses at the barn. *And to think we all thought you would return to train with the Junior Olympic Team.*

*****

Magdalena began zipping up Angie's empty suitcases when she felt a bulge in a side compartment. She opened it to find Angie's big, red diary. She retrieved the book, remembering how Angie had been an inveterate diary keeper since childhood. Magdalena had sometimes read Angie's entries to learn what she was up to next. Taking the book out of the case, she sat on Angie's bed and read what were her eighteen-year-old sister's last days.

Dear Diary,

Just arrived in Molokai to be with Doc. a funky place but he lives here, and I would follow him anywhere. He has a small house on the beach down from the Sheraton. He's the hotel doc. His pad is really bitchin. It's on the sand about two-blocks from the hotel. He says it's old colonial, whatever that means.

I met him on the plane from L.A. I fell for him right away. It was a rough flight, and he gave me some pills that helped my stomach. He stayed at the Royal Hawaiian like our group did. I slipped out of my room the first night to be with him, and the second, and the third. Then he had to go to Molokai for his job, so here I am. I used my American Express card to fly here. I really surprised him when I arrived. But we had another great night of sex.

Magdalena read on, shocked and saddened, wondering how Angie could be so continually reckless.

Dear Diary,

Been here two weeks. Just called home to say this is where I want to live. M is pissed off. I hope she's too busy studying for the bar whatever, to come here. Molokai is kind of barren – sorta like a red desert - Doc Rickman is here and that's all I want.

We've had sex over and over. Unreal! He knows how to do everything in bed and is showing me how to please him. We do coke - drink vodka and Sprite - but don't get too wired. After that, Dear Diary, anything is possible.

Magdalena continued to read how Angie escalated her drug and alcohol use with this man's encouragement. She learned that Rickman sometimes invited other local males to join them, encouraging Angie to use more drugs. He said it brought out the something in her. Angie had badly misspelled the word: *exhibitionism*.

Magdalena collapsed on the bed, swallowing back bile and rubbing her stomach feeling an imminent vomiting attack coming. *Mother of god. Had she been drawn into this outrageous behavior because she grew up without Mama? How did she become so deviant?*

Magdalena returned from the bathroom and sat the book in her lap, stunned and furious. She reread the diary hoping she had misread the seamy parts, but she hadn't. A man over twice Angie's age had used her like a toy. She had complied, and the drugs had taken their relationship to the limits and beyond. This so-called doctor, without doubt, had caused Angie's death.

The door to Angie's room was quietly pushed open by Romulus followed by his brother. Magdalena reached for the mastiffs. Rubbing their massive heads, she said, "Angie's gone boys, and she loved you both so much." Magdalena was sure that she saw understanding in their dark, watery eyes, as they sniffed Angie's diary.

As the dogs settled at Magdalena's feet, she reflected on what the Hawaii Police department had said about where Angie's body was found. It had washed up on the sand in front of the hotel, they said. But clearly, Angie had stayed at night with Rickman, and she had written that his house was down the beach. So, had the tide carried her there from Rickman's place? Magdalena's suspicions grew.

She needed to think, and that meant to swim. She retreated to her room, hid the diary among her law books, and changed into a swimsuit. After being in the pool for over an hour, she emerged after many laps, her thoughts clear.

She contemplated sharing her plan with Sciacca, but wavered mostly against it. But what she would never do was reveal Angie's diary entries to her father. The information would kill him.

Chapter 26

Magdalena walked across the quaint bridge that spanned the lake of the Bel Air Hotel. She slowed where twinkling lights marked her path among large potted gardenias with their soothing aroma. Their sweet scent helped block Angie's funeral from her mind. The grounds seemed even more magical at night. Echoing in the distance, she could hear the piano playing in her destination. She paused at the entrance to the garden room. She so wanted this to be her night, a night she had worked so hard for, a time to celebrate passing the bar. Graduating from Saint Mary's at seventeen, and completing her degree at Loyola college early, meant she could now practice law at the young age of twenty-three. There was no one to share this with but Joseph. Her father had no interest in her life. She could only hope time would one day alter this. Yet why she continued to hope was an enigma to her. She loved her father and respected what he had given up for her and Angie. *Why couldn't he just show me a little love*?

*****

Magdalena approached the garden dining room with no facial makeup, just an application of Revlon Red to her full lips. Her hair, swept high and arranged into the beehive fashion of the day, shone like obsidian. Her thick, dark eyelashes matched the sheen of her hair. When the maître d' approached her, his broad smile and raised eyebrows registered high approval. She stood in a Nehru jacket of dark red brocade that covered her backless white pantsuit. Magdalena's fresh loveliness transcended the heavily made-up beauty of celebrity icons that sprinkled the room. A few Hollywood faces noted her natural, Italian allure. The waiter bowed and said, "Good evening, Miss D' Alessandro. Mr. Cozza is waiting your arrival. Please follow me."

When Magdalena saw the corner table, partially concealed with potted palms, she knew that likely a hundred-dollar bill made this possible, and Joseph had plenty of those. The dining room was appointed in mature plants, canvas covered walls and ceiling that lent an informal coziness to this timeless 1940's hideaway. The hotel radiates an early California aura unlike any other in L.A. Long term Holmby Hills residents and Hollywood royalty claimed it their own for that reason.

"*Buona sera*, Magdalena," Joseph said softly, standing behind her chair. She took a moment to admire him in another of his custom-tailored suits from Milan. He had chosen a shirt and tie of black silk to compliment his camel-colored suit.

Magdalena couldn't help but respond in kind. "*Buona Sera*, Joseph."

Before settling into her chair, she allowed Joseph to help her remove her jacket, revealing her backless pantsuit. The bareness of her back showed no need of a bra, livening his expression and evoking his memory of their night together and her beautiful olive-skinned body.

After softly clearing his throat, he moved his chair closer to hers.

Tommy, the restaurant's most attentive waiter, assigned only to topnotch guests, stood waiting. Magdalena smiled. "Good evening, Tommy, how nice to see you," "I bet Joseph bribed you to wait on us tonight, didn't he?"

Tommy responded with a sheepish smile and a polite bow. "Mr. Cozza maybe suggested it, but it is always a pleasure to serve you, Miss D'Alessandro."

She thought she saw conspiratorial looks between the two. Magdalena envisioned another hundred-dollar bill palmed earlier by Tommy. But if Joseph did spread his money around, it was with a reserve that few Italians in the Organization possessed.

Once seated, Magdalena gazed at Joseph. "This is a special occasion for me."

"It is always a special occasion when I am with you, Magdalena." He turned to signal the wine steward.

Arriving promptly, the dignified sommelier bent to hear Joseph's request. "Mr. Cozza, what can I find for you?"

Magdalena watched Joseph toss the wine list aside. Tell Tommy, the lady would like a dry Martini with two olives," he said turning to confirm the order with Magdalena.

She nodded.

Joseph continued, "I'll have the same, but for dinner I'd like a Gaja Borolo, or if you have it, a Biondi Santi."

The sommelier's eyebrows rose. "For that, I must check my cellar, Mr. Cozza. He disappeared toward the hotel's cache of fine vintages.

With a smile, Joseph turned to her. "Tell me about this special occasion, Magdalena."

She folded her hands on the table, looked up and softly said, "I passed the bar."

"I know you did, and I never doubted that you would." He reached into his jacket pocket and placed a black box before her.

"But how did you know?"

"I just knew," he said pushing his gift closer.

Oh, God, please don't let Joseph give me a ring. She had no jewelry other than a cross that her mother had given her before she died, and Magdalena didn't want what a ring represented.

As she untied the black trim, she read the name imprinted on the ribbon. "Joseph it's from BULGARI!" Magdalena ran her finger over the ribbon with the name of the legendary jewelry house, established in Rome in the 1800's.

"Yes, it is. Let's see if it matches your beauty."

She opened the otter box slowly and felt some relief because the inner case was too large for a ring box.

Magdalena thought she saw the wine steward almost dance to the piano's *Volare* as he returned with a dusty bottle of wine. "Will this be to your liking, Mr. Cozza?"

Even Joseph's reserve faltered when he saw the 1945 Bioni Santi vintage, "Yes. Yes, that's excellent."

"I'll decant the bottle and return shortly, Sir."

Magdalena knew Joseph was watching her open his gift. She stopped opening the gift when he put his hand on hers and said, "I want this to be the beginning of many gifts I give you, Magdalena." When the wine steward returned, decanter in hand, Joseph put up a hand to ward him off for this special moment. The steward retreated a few steps back. "Please, Magdalena." He nodded to her to continue opening the gift.

She raised the lid from the velvet case. "Oh, Joseph, these are magnificent ruby earrings! You must have paid a fortune for them. I've never received such a gift."

Joseph sat back in his chair with an expression of satisfaction. "I have a very old auntie who always says, if you're a man who loves a woman enough, you give her 'Bulgari.'"

Magdalena didn't know how to respond to Joseph's comment, and held her head down, her eyes shadowed with her thick lashes. Joseph signaled the sommelier to step forward, and relished the pouring and the color of the rich red wine. Magdalena sipped her Martini and admired her new earrings. She held up one to the table candle. When the *Biondi Santi* was poured into a large glass, Magdalena sighed, "Look Joseph, the wine matches my ruby earrings perfectly."

*****

The Swan Lake Suite had been Joseph's choice for their night together. Once in their room, Magdalena stepped onto the terrace to watch the two regal birds, one black one white, glide silently across the pond. She felt Joseph wrap his arms around her. "They say these birds mate for life, Magdalena," he whispered in her ear. She gently slipped out of his embrace, not interested in where the conversation was headed. "Joseph, I have a few questions."

Joseph wrinkled his brow and reached for his cigarette case. She watched him sit and study her in silence. "And what would your questions be, Magdalena?" he asked, searching his pockets for his lighter.

"Did the Organization lend money to the land company that developed the Sheraton Hotel in Molokai?"

Joseph relaxed a little. "Where did that question come from?"

"Please Joseph, just answer."

"Yeah, maybe. Right now, like now we're loaning

money to get Las Vegas hotels going. It's one of our businesses. Why?"

Magdalena didn't answer him. "And would you or Jimmy know of anyone who might work at that hotel now?"

"Maybe. I'd have to look into that. Why?"

"I've decided I want to see where Angie spent her last days. As a matter of fact, I'm going to leave tomorrow for the Islands.

Joseph sat stone-faced after she spoke about leaving tomorrow. Before he could ask her anything else, Magdalena bent down to his chair. She removed the cigarette from his hand, and sat on his lap. Then she gave him a big kiss, almost as erotic as the one she gave him after her father's stroke. Magdalena remained in his lap doing what she liked best, being held and kissed. Soon they were undressing one another and moving to the bed where their lovemaking quickly became passionate. For the balance of the evening, Magdalena seduced Joseph with a sexual abandon that would surprise, and almost confuse him. He would come to learn that Magdalena's lovemaking was akin to therapy, and was not about her partner.

Chapter 27

Joseph checked out of the Bel Air and drove west down Sunset Blvd., a road that winds down to the ocean like a giant snake. His troubled expression indicated he was going over in his mind his conversation with Magdalena. After swinging into a beach parking lot and stepping from his car, Joseph stood rummaging in his pockets for change.

The floor of the phone booth was gritty with sand and the receiver greasy with what smelled liked sun tan oil. “Hello, Sciacca,” Joseph said quickly. “I just left Magdalena, and she’s flying to Hawaii as we speak. If I didn’t know better, I’d think she was going there for *venganza*.”

“Slow down and explain,” said Sciacca.

“I spent the night with her at the Bel Air, and she said in just a few words that she wanted to investigate something about Angie’s death. But she’s so damn secretive, it’s tough getting any real facts from her.”

“Do we know where she’s staying?”

“The Royal Hawaiian, but she asked me if we had a contact at the Sheraton Molokai. My guess is that she’ll fly there soon. That’s where her sister died.

*****

Soon after takeoff an agile TWA stewardess moved

about the first cabin offering cocktails, wines and hors d'oeuvres. "I'll have a Bloody Mary and a shrimp cocktail," Magdalena said. Then she cracked open her new book by Steven King, *The Dead Zone*, a weird author everyone said, but she was happy just to read for leisure for a change. Not long after, she was offered a pillow and a blanket. She closed her book and slept through most of the flight. When she awoke, it was to the voice of a southern gentleman next to her. She turned sleepy-eyed to the man.

Patting her hand, he said, "Safety belts on, Missy. The pilot's about to land this big bird."

*****

Once settled in her room at the Royal Hawaiian, Magdalena asked the operator to place a call to Los Angeles. She needed to talk to Sciacca. Any information he had about the Molokai hotel and its staff, especially it's doctor, would be helpful. And she had to admit that being in Sciacca's company, or even on the phone with him, had a settling effect on her. His pleasant and avuncular manner made her feel valued. Checking the hotel drink list while waiting for her mainland connection, she decided on a Royal Hawaiian cocktail, labeled a complimentary beverage. A waiter soon arrived with a tall glass garnished with a pineapple cube, a maraschino cherry, a miniature orchid and an umbrella.

She liked the languid feeling of Hawaii, and took her drink to the balcony where she enjoyed the humid air and the blazing sunset. Relaxed on her chaise lounge, she sipped from the straw and examined the crowded topping of her drink. A minute insect had fallen from the orchid into the cocktail and was working to avoid drowning. She stared into the distance, *venganza* in her eyes.

The first ring of the phone quickly ended her trance,

and picking up the receiver, she heard an operator's voice. "Your party is on the line, Miss D'Alessandro."

"Hello, Jimmy," she said.

"Magdalena, tell me what you are doing in Hawaii, alone."

"I need to settle some business here that relates to my sister's death, Jimmy."

Sciacca was silent for a few moments. "How can I help?"

"I'm used to working with a private investigator when I want information, like Papa's P.I., Harold. And here…"

"I understand completely, you need a little inside information."

"Exactly, Jimmy."

"OK, I need to make a few calls, and I'll get back to you tomorrow. I'll call back about this time. But listen to me, Magdalena, I want my only goddaughter to be very careful."

"Yes sir, I plan to."

*****

The following day, after talking with Sciacca, Magdalena took the twenty-minute flight to Molokai. As the small plane banked over the island, the view of the land reminded her of Angie's diary description - "sorta like a red desert." The grounds of the new Sheraton occupied a peninsula, that included an expansive golf course. From the air, it appeared the only beauty spot on the whole island. She had reserved a corner suite at the hotel, with an open-ended checkout date. She hoped it was a refuge from this uninviting, arid place. She checked in as Maggie Mancuso.

*****

At sunset, Magdalena walked slowly into the cocktail lounge. Her black shining hair fell loose around her shoulders. Her floral sarong, bought in the hotel gift shop, flowed over her body as she moved. A Hawaiian woman at the entrance to the lounge offered her a lei. "Aloha," the woman said placing the white mini orchards around her neck.

"Thank you," Magdalena said, then remained standing in place as though she wanted a table rather than a seat at the bar.

Shortly after the bartender noticed the Italian beauty, he slipped under his bar top to approach, not something he did often. "Would you like to dine in the lounge, Miss?"

"Yes, actually, I'd rather have my dinner here than in the dining room. Is that possible?"

"Of course," he said, reaching for a dinner menu.

"I'd like that far corner table," Magdalena said with a soft but confident voice. As she sat adjusting her sarong to reveal a leg, she was aware of the bartender trying, without success, not to ogle her.

"I won't be needing this," Magdalena said as she handed the menu back, yet not releasing it. "May I ask your name?"

"Ah, yes." He cleared his throat. "It's Tony."

"Tony, do we have a mutual friend?"

"Yeah, I think so, a Mr. S?" Tony said cautiously.

Magdalena released the menu and nodded, with a brief smile.

"Can I get you a cocktail, Miss?"

"Please, make me one of those Hawaiian drinks, but not too sweet, and you may call me Maggie." The secrecy of her visit, her inside man Tony and her new name all appealed to Magdalena. After bowing to her as though she represented Hawaiian royalty, Tony was off to blend the perfect drink. When he returned Magdalena ordered her dinner: a Caesar salad, a blood-rare filet mignon and a baked potato.

For four nights, her dinner order didn't alter, and she always sat at the same corner table. In her first week at the hotel, she had come to be the guest most everyone talked about, especially the men. Golfers discussed her on the greens. Employees followed her movement with a curious interest. Offers to pay for her food and drink were frequent among male guests. One man even sent her a note offering her his hundred-foot yacht for as long as she liked.

It was clear Magdalena had her own money, and this intrigued the males that danced around her. Their inquisitiveness was unlimited. The men who inquired after her found they had to go through Tony, and he was an effective gatekeeper. The number of inquiries Tony received about her genuinely amused Magdalena bringing to mind Gloria Steinem's quote: 'If you're single and have your own support, you must be hooking.'

At dinner hour in the lounge, on the fourth evening of her stay, a man Tony greeted as 'Doc' took a seat at the bar. That name and face suppressed Magdalena's appetite. 'Doc' didn't approach her or offer to buy her a drink. He didn't even ogle her, which was actually a bit of a relief.

Leaning across the bar, Doctor Richard Shaw spoke quietly, "So who's the chick in the sarong, a high-class hooker?"

"No, man. She's just a guest here on her own."

Chapter 28

Magdalena found the outdoor pool at the Sheraton warm and inviting. The water beckoned her to rise early and return to the regimen of her morning swim. Near sunrise, she mistakenly took the service elevator down to the pool, greeting two hotel maids with a smile as she entered. At a midway stop, Doc Shaw stepped in to the elevator attempting to smooth his ruffled hair, and tuck in his shirt. The maids covered their smiles, and lapsed into Spanish. Magdalena grasped enough of their language to know they were gossiping about the womanizing hotel doctor.

Shaw attempted a boyish grin.

Magdalena regarded him with cold eyes and turned away.

"Down for a swim?" he asked.

Knowing she had to conceal her loathing, Magdalena turned back to him with a nod and a cool smile. She was relieved when he exited. She didn't want to meet him this way. Her pool sandals would expose her limp, and she couldn't possibly allow him that view of her. Not yet.

When Magdalena arrived at the pool, she swam more laps than usual. This had always been her private time, where she laid plans, solved problems and reviewed her mistakes. While swimming, she thought of the P.I. Sciacca had promised her. She was glad it had turned out to be Tony, whom she found easy to talk with. But between Angie's diary and her own instincts, she didn't have a lot to ask Tony to investigate. Perhaps he would play a part in her plan later.

When she climbed the pool steps to leave, a lifeguard approached. "I was instructed to give you this personally, Miss Mancuso," he said, setting an envelope on a lounge chair.

She saw Maggie written on the outside as she reached for a towel. Thinking it was Shaw making a play for her, she casually opened the note and read a few scribbled words. 'Your father has been moved to a nursing home. Call Mr. S.' It was signed Tony.

Magdalena sat alone at the steps to the pool until the lifeguard, noticing how despondent she appeared, approached. "Are you all right, Miss?"

Magdalena shook her head, not wanting to speak. She left and headed toward the elevator. Once in her room, she slammed the door and fell onto her bed. She wanted to see Papa, talk to him, tell him she was going to avenge Angie's death and most of all tell him that she loved him. Her sister's death had nearly taken her father's life. Magdalena muffled her crying with her pillow.

I know you loved Angie more than me because she looked like Mama. And when you overheard me talking to Sciacca you eliminated me from your life. I had to swim hundreds of laps to figure that out, Papa. But I still love you and will do everything in my power to keep you well.

Magdalena fell into a sound sleep and didn't wake until early evening, feeling guilty that she hadn't called Sciacca. Then looking at herself in the mirror, she saw puffy eyes, red checks and matted hair.

Magdalena soon got the desk on the phone and asked for a massage and a facial as soon as possible.

"Of course, Miss D'Alessandro. Would you like to come down now? We have a masseuse available."

"Yes, I just have to place a call and I'll be down.

*****

"Hello, Magdalena, I'm sorry you had to be away when this happened," Sciacca said switching on his speaker phone, and motioning to Joseph to listen.

Her voice came out shaky over the phone. "I'm sure you did the right thing, Jimmy. How is Papa?"

Frown lines on Sciacca's face reflected her sad voice. Joseph had begun to pace the room with a set jaw while fumbling for a cigarette.

"Your father is in no pain, Magdalena, and I moved him to the finest nursing home in Beverly Hills. He needs professional care, now, Magdalena. Will this change your plans?" asked Sciacca.

"No, but I will accelerate what I want to do here. Give me another week or two. And I promise to call daily about Papa."

Crumbling the unlit cigarette in his palm and beginning to pace again, Joseph's exasperation almost forced him to ask Sciacca to speak to Magdalena.

"Then I'll be waiting for my goddaughter to return home safe. Okay?" Sciacca said.

"Yes, I will be careful, Jimmy. I promise." She placed the phone in the cradle.

"She's going to bump him." Joseph said plopping into a chair. "But how?" He looked at Sciacca. "Do you want me to go over and do him before she can get herself in trouble?

*****

After her massage and facial, Magdalena felt renewed. Sitting at her corner table in the lounge for dinner, she appeared calm and beautiful again. Her olive skin glistened, her hair was piled high and stylish. Yet she couldn't shake her melancholy due to her father's decline. Her thoughts were random and coming in waves. Should she fly home and see her father? Had she arranged for flowers to be sent to the vase at Angie's crypt? Had she packed the altered shoes she needed? Then Joseph popped into her thoughts. *It would be nice to have him waiting in my room tonight*. But the plan that she had developed while swimming laps at sunrise soon took precedence.

When Tony approached her with her dinner tray, he too, had a sorrowful look. "Sorry about your father, Maggie," he said softly. "Mr. S. had to tell me so I would track you down immediately. Are you flying home?"

"Thank you, Tony." She shook her head, "No, I'm not going home just yet. My father's health has been failing for some time, and he's been moved into a nursing home where he will get the best care."

As Tony set Magdalena's entree before her and removed the domed lid, he stood as though waiting for orders. Magdalena decided to put her plan into action. "I was reading the hotel newsletter about that old wooden ship in the bay."

"Yeah," he perked. "The Doc and I...," he stopped in mid-sentence. "Do you know Doc Shaw?"

Magdalena shook her head.

"He's the hotel doctor. He and I were just talking about that old square-rigger just last night. A crew member fell from the rigging and broke a leg yesterday. They brought him to the hotel for the Doc to see."

"Really? is the man okay?"

"He's fine. Crew are usually tough," he smiled.

"How far out would you say the ship is?"

"Maybe a hundred yards. Those old clippers, like the Regina Maris have deep drafts and they have to moor pretty far out."

"You sound like you know old ships."

"Well, I know this one. I crewed on her once. She's a turn-of-the-century clipper, built in Scandinavia and carries six thousand square feet of sail."

Magdalena carved into her blood-rare steak while noting Tony's fascination with the old ship. "I'd like to swim out to it before I leave Molokai."

"I don't think that would be possible. She's a little too far out."

Magdalena smiled and nodded as she chewed her steak.

"Hey, here comes Shaw now. Would you like to meet him?"

When Magdalena saw Shaw, she prematurely swallowed her meat. "Yes," she said, swallowing hard then clearing her throat.

"Maggie, meet Doc Shaw," Tony said, waving Shaw to the table.

Chapter 29

Magdalena hadn't met many handsome professionals but he qualified. Tall, almost gangly with lots of black hair, he affected a jock-like carriage. With his easy smile, and his boyish tilt to his head, she knew he looked younger than his age. He should be sporting some grey, she thought. She decided his ego had remedied that. As he came closer his stride betrayed a forced self-esteem. Although he exuded charm she loathed looking into his eyes, which told another story. They couldn't conceal his callousness, but she stared into them, knowing it would help her execute her plan.

****

"Hello, Mr. Sciacca, it's Tony at the Sheraton in Molokai."

"What's up, Tony."

"Well, you told me to contact you when Magdalena got together with someone, and she did tonight. It's the hotel doctor."

"What do you mean 'got together'?" Sciacca asked.

"I just mean they had dinner together. I introduced them. But if you mean did they go to her suite or his house, no I don't think so."

"Do you know if they talked about anything in particular?"

"Yeah, there's an old clipper ship in the bay, and that's what they talked about."

"That's it?"

"Yes sir, that's about it. But she did talk about swimming out to see it."

"Alone?" Sciacca asked.

"I told her it was too far out to swim. Okay, and one other thing sir, she refers to herself here as Maggie, checked in as Maggie Mancuso."

*****

Magdalena passed the lounge late the next afternoon and noticed that Tony was starting his shift. She had been at the Sheraton about a week and hadn't been able to talk to him alone. The lounge was empty, so she took a seat at the bar. "Hi, Maggie, how's it going?"

"Good, I'm getting a little too used to this indolent living though."

"You'll have to tell me what that word means, Maggie."

She smiled. "Tony, you know Mr. S. indicated you could give me background on someone."

Tony nodded.

"I need any info you have on Doc Shaw."

Tony came close, setting her Hawaiian beverage before her, and speaking softly. "He's been the hotel doc for nearly four years. He has a wife on the mainland, goes there almost never. Usually makes the rounds with women who stay in the hotel, especially the young ones. The broads love him."

Magdalena nodded pensively. "I know all that, anything else?"

"Yeah, he asks a lot of questions about you."

*****

Soon Shaw began spending evenings with the woman he knew as Maggie. Her quiet style, beauty and brains set her apart from women he usually pursued. Her interest in early morning swimming had intrigued him, particularly after she explained it had started with polio rehabilitation as a young girl. His curiosity got the better of him about this regimen of hers.

Walking down the beach from his cottage, not long after sunrise the following morning, Shaw arrived at the hotel pool. "Hi, Ben, where's the woman who usually does laps in the morning?" Shaw asked the lifeguard.

"You mean Maggie? She left earlier with Doug. It's his day off, and when she saw his outrigger club meeting here, she asked if she could go with them. They didn't have much objection."

"So where did they go?" Shaw asked.

"I think they wanted to cruise around that old ship out there in the bay."

****

After her day at sea with the outrigger club, Magdalena took a long nap and didn't wake until early evening. That night, when she entered the lounge, she looked rested and vivacious. An afternoon breathing salt air and soaking up male attention had its advantages.

Shaw was seated at her table, fidgeting with his scotch, drumming his fingers. She couldn't help but be amused to see him actually stand at her arrival. Her guess was he didn't do that often. "Nice to see you arrive. We thought you may have gone off with a Polynesian sailor," Shaw said, a hint of jealously in his voice.

Magdalena took a seat, looking relaxed. With her, she brought the aroma of plumeria perfume, a floral scent from the islands. "It was my best day here, yet," Magdalena said.

"I got to paddle with the outrigger club."

She turned to Tony who had just arrived to take their dinner order. "We cruised out to the old wooden ship that you crewed on,"

"Isn't she something?" Tony said. "Did you go aboard?"

"No, we were invited but the club wanted to paddle, and that's what we did." What an exhilarating experience it is, going to sea in one of those native canoes."

Tony's head bobbed with enthusiasm. "And I have never seen them take a woman cannoning," he said.

Magdalena flashed him one of her rare smiles. "And as a result, I'm starved Tony. Please order my usual. And no Hawaiian punches tonight. Would you bring me a bottle of your best red wine?"

"Will do, Maggie."

Sober-faced, Shaw said, "I'll take a surf 'n' turf," then turned away from Tony.

Magdalena went on about her experience on the outrigger for the better part of the evening. Like a sailor smitten by the sea, she waxed on about the romance and beauty of ocean seafaring.

Shaw sat like an observer, evidently trying to figure out this beauty who had traveled alone to Molokai - the backwater of the Hawaiian Islands.

Magdalena watched Shaw try to listen with interest to her day. She knew he didn't give a damn. With each scotch, he was less able to conceal his boredom with her subject. Staying reasonably sober, sipping little of her wine, gave Magdalena an advantage. She found it interesting to thwart him when he began attempts at intimacy.

"You've been here well over a week, Maggie, and I haven't even shown you where I live." He ran his hand up her arm. "There's a full moon tonight. that would light our walk down the beach to my place," he said. "It's just down the beach," he repeated.

Looking across the table at him, Magdalena's eyes shown bright in the candlelight, then narrowed. "That's right, you have an old colonial cottage on the sand, don't you?"

With a smirk on his face, Shaw nodded. "Who told you about my house? Your sister, Angie?" Shaw said slumped back in his chair.

Magdalena was shocked when she heard Shaw refer to Angie as her sister. She rose from the table and rushed to the elevator. Her hands shook when she hit the button to her floor. Rushing down the hall to her room, she fumbled her key into the door lock then ran to the bathroom, getting there just in the nick of time. Standing over the toilet, she stared at her vomit. *Shaw knows me.*

Magdalena had calculated that this could happen, even though she registered under a false last name. But when it did, it created a fear in her she hadn't anticipated. She had to get a hold of herself. He couldn't possibly know her plans.

She had heard that men say to hold your enemy close. *Why was it so hard to do the same?* For a moment, she felt her resolve weaken. Then she collected her thoughts and decided this panic was of her own making. She would move forward with her plan by gaining Shaw's trust, and make him malleable. Knowing he viewed her as another conquest would be an advantage. She would lengthen the chase.

Magdalena's instincts told her to avoid Shaw for a few days. She needed recovery time from having been exposed. She knew it was natural to fear one's enemy. But she reminded herself that he was her prey, not her predator, plus she was on a timetable. She had promised Sciacca that she would be home in one or two weeks, and she would keep her word.

Chapter 30

Magdalena thought of a way to disappear for a few days. She slipped into the bar the next afternoon to talk to Tony about her escape. "Tony, I need a favor."

"Boy, you sure flew out of here last night. Everything okay?"

"Yes," she said, quickly moving on. "Remember the guy that offered me his yacht?"

"Yeah. He's still here, playing golf."

"Can you arrange a charter for me on his yacht? And when you do, see that I get the boat to myself."

"Yeah, I think I can. He's rich as they come, and it's a pristine motor sailor. She's a hundred feet, carries a crew of five. The captain was in the other night, hell of a nice guy."

Tony always wanted to talk about the specifications of boats and the number of crewmembers.

"Olay, okay, please arrange that I have the boat to myself for three days. Tell him I just want the crew to sail me around the island.

"All by yourself?"

"Yes, Tony, by myself."

Soon after Tony arranged for Magdalena to charter the yacht, he called Sciacca. "Hello, Sir. It's Tony. You said you wanted to know when Maggie did something out of the ordinary. Well, I just thought you would like to know that she has chartered a yacht for three days, and she was stubborn about no guests."

"How big is this boat?"

"She's well over a hundred feet."

"And she gave no reason why is she going on this boat?"

"No reason, Sir."

"Is it a safe boat?"

"Very safe, Sir – a full crew."

"Okay, let's talk when she returns," Sciacca said.

When Sciacca hung up the phone, a lovesick Joseph arrived with his daily request. "Just send me to the Islands. *I'll* bump the guy and bring her back." He asked and punched out a cigarette on a crystal ashtray in Sciacca's office.

Not a rash man, Sciacca took time to respond. "Sit down, Joseph," he said quietly.

Joseph did as he was told.

"Listen to me. The heat is all over our territories. This new Police Chief, Daryl Gates, is running L.A. with a new hammer. He calls it the SWAT team. And the Attorney General, John Van De Kamp, is on a fucking mission to wipe out what he calls 'career criminals.' They're looking into all our operations: drugs, porn, loan sharking, even the tracks. And you, you want to go to the Islands and save Magdalena, like a, hero!"

Frowning, Joseph attempted a rebuttal. "I just thought that I could get this out of the way for you, boss."

"This is what you will do, Joseph. Call Salvatore and have him clip this doc that Magdalena has such a hard on for."

"Salvatore the Horse? But he's old school, and I

could…"

The dark look on Sciacca's face halted a response from Joseph. Soon he was in the other room calling Salvatore, the Horse.

*****

The next night, Tony tended a slow bar while Shaw downed scotches and went on about Magdalena. "She chartered that motor sailor, didn't she? What the hell for? Does she have a thing for the captain?" Shaw didn't wait for answers; he just fired questions.

"I don't know, but she sure shot out of here last night," Tony said busying himself washing glasses.

Shaw looked annoyed. "You got any cigarettes?"

"Here," Tony said, tossing him a pack of Camels. "Someone left these behind."

As Shaw lit up and drank more scotch, his talk became less clear.

"Party in the dining room?" Shaw said swiveling his bar stool toward the noise.

"Some chick is celebrating her eighteenth birthday," Tony said.

"Really, I'll have to check her out."

"Some things never change," Tony muttered under his breath.

Shaw downed another scotch. "Why do you suppose she's here, I mean really here? Do you think she blames me for her sister's death? Jesus, Angie was a loose cannon. You knew that. Right?" Shaw rambled.

Toni had been paid by Sciacca to listen, not talk, so it was easy not to answer Shaw's rhetorical questions.

******

The motor yacht Magdalena had chartered maneuvered toward the Sheraton dock. The crew secured the boat as

Magdalena stood onboard, viewing the hotel beach. Well beyond that stretch of sand was Shaw's cottage. Shading her eyes, she could make out his residence: a colonial wooden frame house, just as Angie had described it.

Magdalena's private inquiry and Angie's diary strongly suggested that her sister died in that cottage. Magdalena knew in her gut that Angie was put in the surf, her death made to appear as a drowning. The Hawaiian police reported cocaine in Angie's system. She didn't get that from the sea.

Magdalena had hired a P.I. who found nothing that could be used in a court of law, let alone any evidence that hinted Shaw could have been directly responsible for Angie's death. Evidently cocaine was in use throughout the islands, so the amount in Angie's blood drew no special interest from the police.

With Magdalena's intense need for privacy, she chose not to share her supposition with anyone. She couldn't tell her father what her investigation dredged up. It would kill him, and he probably wouldn't believe her. If she told Joseph, he would want to become involved. Magdalena wasn't quite sure why she didn't want to confide in Sciacca in this matter. But after Angie's funeral, she had decided that her sister's death would be avenged. She would do it for Papa, even if he never knew, and she would do it for Angie. Punitive action by the law was rarely quick and too often unobtainable.

Stepping off the boarding ladder onto the pier, Magdalena looked refreshed and lustrous, her olive skin aglow from her radiant face to her polished toes. "Thank you, Captain, for three glorious days of cruising."

"You are most welcome, Miss. You're a good sailor," said the captain.

Her big smile and beauty bedazzled the crew who were leaning on the ship's railing for a last glimpse of her. Wearing a long sarong, with her black hair flowing in the ocean breeze, she walked the landing to the hotel. Her beach sandals exposed her limp, which for the first time in her memory simply didn't concern her.

As she walked along the dock, she sighed, relieved that her reason for coming to Molokai was clear again and her confidence regained. There was Shaw at the end of the wharf flirting with a young, female crewmember. Magdalena slowed her walk until Shaw saw her.

Rushing toward her, he produced a lei. "You look great, Maggie. The sea really agrees with you," he said ignoring the young woman.

When he placed the strand of flowers around her neck, Magdalena could feel the intensity of his desire. She could also smell scotch.

He suspects nothing. She smiled at him.

"I do love the sea. I think I could live on the water," Magdalena said seeing an innocent reply coming. *He wants to tell me something.*

"Maggie, I wanted to say sorry about mentioning your sister the other night." His words were without sincerity.

Perfect timing, thought Magdalena. "Yes, it made me sad. I think that's why I had to get away for a few days."

"Yeah, I apologize," he said again showing little contrition.

Magdalena reached under her dark glasses to wipe away a tear that wasn't there. She spoke softly. "It's hard talking about her."

Looking at the ground, Shaw stopped talking.

They were silent as they headed toward the lobby.

When the hotel elevator opened, Magdalena stepped in.

Shaw held the door. Magdalena removed her sunglasses.

"Anything I can do to make amends, Maggie?" said Shaw with a sexual gleam in his eyes.

He doesn't know me at all, thought Magdalena. "Shaw, I know you had an affair with my sister. And I know you were drunk when you mentioned her the other night. Let's forget about all of that. I don't want to feel that pain anymore. I came here because I just wanted to return to Angie's last place of happiness," Magdalena said with words that sounded sincere even to her.

Shaw's face shone with lust. "Let me take you somewhere, let's do something. Tonight!"

Magdalena found her sexy voice. "Not tonight, but I would really like to go aboard that old clipper ship that's moored in the bay tomorrow, maybe even swim out to it."

*****

Salvatore the Horse, was on the next flight to Honolulu after receiving his assignment from Sciacca. He flew Pan Am, first class, and resembled a fat sausage packed into his aircraft seat. "Hey, Stew, how about a martini with a couple of olives?" his surly voice grated, as he groped the stewardess with his eyes.

"Right away, Sir," she said giving a co-worker the 'oh brother look.' "What cave did he crawl out of?" she whispered in the galley.

*****

The next morning Magdalena got Shaw's house phone number from Tony, who reminded her that Shaw had really waded into the scotch last night. *All the better*, thought Magdalena. *He'll lack energy and endurance*. She called him in the early morning.

"Good morning. Ready for our outing?"

With a raspy voice, Shaw said, "What? Who is this?"

"You don't know who this is?" Magdalena said in her sexy voice.

"Ah, sure, it's just early. What time is it anyway?"

"Time to get an outboard and go to the bay where that old clipper ship is moored. Remember?"

"Sure. When do you want to go?"

"Now. I'm picking up lunch. You rent the outboard. Meet you at the dock in thirty minutes." She hung up.

*****

"Yeah, yeah, I know how to handle an outboard, Doug. We'll be fine."

"Sorry Doc. Just wanted to give you a few pointers," said the rental dock-hand. Magdalena smiled secretly.

The hotel kept two outboard boats. It was the most common way of allowing guests to motor about the bay, but ordinarily with an attendant.

"Well, don't," said a cranky, hung-over Shaw.

As they set out, the outboard lurched when Shaw worked the throttle lever, nearly throwing Magdalena from the boat.

"Sorry," he said, as he headed toward the small bay where the square-rigger lay anchored. She watched Shaw eye the clipper ship. "Let's go to the old boat first, then to the bay? They'll let us come on board, especially the way you're dressed."

His words were snide, not complimentary, and Magdalena drew her beach wrap together to cover her bikini. She felt a tinge of fear. She told herself that she was getting a view of Shaw that would make her plan easier. As he began weaving the outboard dangerously, she gathered he was making some kind of macho statement. Sitting at the bow, Magdalena gripped the sides of the small craft, her hair flying. She was determined not to show the fear she felt. The wind made it hard to speak. "I want us to lounge on the beach together," she called, anxious for him to slow down.

"Okay, but I'm going to make a lap around your old boat. What's her name? Oh yeah there it is, Regina Maris," he said, accelerating the small craft. Magdalena thought he delighted in frightening her as he made reckless turns circling the old clipper.

"Hey, old man," came a voice from someone on deck. "Easy, or you'll dump that outboard."

"Fuck you," Shaw said under his breath as he headed toward the bay, continuing to ramp up speed. When they arrived at the cove, it was with too much speed. The boat hit the sand hard and lurched, throwing Magdalena forward. She landed face down in the bottom of the craft. Her mouth was bleeding when she sat up.

"Oh Jesus, let me take a look at that," Shaw said, his first sincere words all morning.

Magdalena held her head high, and remained silent as he examined her. "It's a superficial cut. You just bit your lip. Let me put some salt water on it."

Magdalena remained still as Shaw dabbed her lip with a wet towel. "I apologize," he said.

Magdalena stood, stepped over the lunch that was strewn across the bottom of the boat, reached for her beach bag and in silence headed for the sand. She spread out her towel to lie on but wasn't sure how to proceed. The relaxed mood she had planned wasn't going to happen. Shaw and his hangover had been in control ever since they started out. And she couldn't let go of the sharp comment he had made about her scant bikini. It disturbed her, and made her realize his negative attitude toward women was hateful. She had to think of what to do next. Stuck at this somewhat distant location with a man she knew was responsible for her sister's death, she began to worry. The closest people were on the clipper ship, and they weren't even within calling distance. She felt Shaw flop on the sand next to her, and felt uneasy about his next move. She was greatly relieved when she heard him snoring, dealing with that hangover.

Magdalena retrieved a small umbrella from the boat and salvaged what was left of their lunch. She set up the shade to cover him, deciding that she wanted him asleep as long as possible. Maybe after sleeping, he would wake less angry from his hangover. Sitting on her towel, she thought, *what a beautiful place to be with such a worthless man.* Too bad he couldn't be Joseph when he woke up. She shook her head to clear those thoughts, stood and headed for the water.

Magdalena had never swum in the ocean and found it a pleasure, especially in this calm bay. She found herself more buoyant and the taste of the salt appealing. She floated leisurely, looking up at the cloudless sky.

Shaw is here only because he thinks he thinks he's going to have sex with me. To date I have avoided that, but I know I can't any longer. He's going to wake and want me here and now. My original plan to get him to swim out to the old ship won't work now. I have got to somehow use sex.

She began to tread water and looked toward the bay to check on Shaw. He was standing, waving his arms like he was bringing in a plane. "Hey, let's have some lunch," he called.

His hangover must be talking to his stomach, she thought. "Let's first have a dip?" she called back.

"Okay, okay," he said walking half-heartedly into the gentle surf.

Continuing to tread water, Magdalena moved her arms to distance her from Shaw. "It's really beautiful out here.

Did you know I have never been in the ocean before?" she called to him.

"Yeah, well I'm a good swimmer. When I moved to Molokai, I swam every morning in the ocean. Kinda got out of the habit though."

I'll bet you did, you scotch guzzling sot. She egged him on. "Come on out where it's a little deeper and cooler."

"I'm coming," he said, with a little more enthusiasm.

As he entered the water, she could see, he had exaggerated his swimming prowess. He flapped like an albatross in the water. She began to improvise a plan. Magdalena slipped out of her bathing suit top and tucked it into the bottom, then called in a maiden-in-distress voice. "Oh, no!"

"What?" Shaw said looking up from swimming.

"My top has come off and I can't find it."

"I'll be right there," he said eagerly. He got a sudden burst of energy.

Magdalena continued to lengthen the distance between them. "Oh, look, I found it," she said, holding the top in midair.

He swam toward her vigorously for only a few minutes longer. Magdalena heard his short, quick breathing. "Maggie, let's go back," he said, gasping.

"Go back! We're nearly half way to the ship. Let's swim to it?"

Shaw stopped swimming to tread water. With effort, he worked his arms to keep his head up. "Don't be ridiculous; we'd never make it. Come on, I'm serious. We've come too far. I'm going back."

She saw him turn his head from the ship and back to shore. His frightened expression revealed that he saw he was beyond midway, incapable of returning to the shore.

His confidence left him. He struggled for words. “Maggie, swim over to me. Help me get back to shore.”

Magdalena looked at him with a dead stare. “Why?” she asked.

Shaw went under momentarily, then surfaced sputtering and yelling. “Why? Because I need you to save me.”

“But I don’t want to save you,” she said in a flat tone.

“Maggie, for Christ sake. Help me?” Shaw made an failed attempt to turn around and head for the shore. With that effort, he disappeared again, and when he got his head above water a second time, his words were desperate. “My legs are cramping, I need help.”

Magdalena watched Shaw vanish one more time. She waited until she knew he had drowned. With easy, slow strokes she swam to the Regina Maris. She paused at the boarding ladder to rest a few minutes, and thought briefly of Angie. When she called for help, she surprised herself at how distraught she sounded.

Chapter 31

Salvatore the Horse, was on his way toward the lobby of the Molokai Sheraton when a commotion at the back of the hotel drew his attention. Paramedics and police were all over the place. Hotel management was trying desperately to downplay or conceal the disturbance. Salvatore stood, unnoticed, watching the uproar. A policewoman had wrapped a towel and an arm around an attractive, olive-skinned woman in a bikini who needed help standing. Swiftly and discretely, paramedics slid a body in their van. Salvatore left to enter the hotel and find the bar.

"You Tony?" graveled Salvatore.

Tony nodded.

"Make me a martini with two olives."

"Coming right up," Tony said, wondering how this guy could be a tourist.

"What's going on out back?" growled Salvatore.

"Ah, a man drowned," Tony uttered.

With a crocked smile, Salvatore asked, "Oh, yeah? Was it the hotel doc?"

Tony's stared at the unlikely tourist, shocked. "Who are you?"

"I'm Salvatore. Sciacca sent me," he said, staring into his empty martini glass and shaking his head. "She beat me to it. She's gotta be Sicilian!"

*****

Magdalena drove down Stone Canyon to the Bel Air Hotel to meet Sciacca for lunch. She had been back from Molokai a month. The police had released her, calling Shaw's death accidental.

She walked across the bridge to look for the swans and found them surrounded by their companions, the ducks. They were all feeding on the daily loaf of bread a waiter had thrown their way.

Moving on to the garden room for lunch, passing the giant bougainvillea, she wondered why Sciacca wanted to meet with her in the dining room, and saw him at the table where they had often met.

"You are looking lovely, Magdalena," he said as he stood at their table to greet her.

"Thank you, Jimmy." she could see he was distracted by someone behind her. She turned to see a serene looking blond woman with two men at a table in the middle of the room.

"You see who that is, Magdalena?" He said with delight. "I just sent her table a Dom Perignon. He offered a small wave toward the woman like an awestruck child.

"Yes. I think I do. Isn't it Grace Kelly?" Magdalena was both embarrassed and amused by Sciacca's fascination with the movie star. But she had heard secretly he loved to be around Hollywood people, and that was why he dined and often stayed at the hotel.

Sciacca's face turned serious. "I'm glad you learned to called me, 'Jimmy,' Magdalena. My first name is actually Dominic, but I've always been called Jimmy."

Magdalena's expression grew sad. "That's my father's first name."

"Yes, I know. How is your father?"

"The same, Sir, I mean Jimmy."

Sciacca lit a small cigar. "Magdalena, I'll just say this once. You did good in the Islands avenging your sister. If it had been my sister, I would have done the same. But I want your word that if something like this comes up again, you call me first. Understand?"

"Yes," Magdalena answered wide-eyed. *He knows. I guess I knew he would find out but, now what...?*

Sciacca rolled his cigar between his thumb and forefinger. "But that's not why I wanted to talk to you."

Magdalena felt a relief mixed with curiosity.

"You have taken over all the cases we have given you and handled them just as professionally as your father did."

She nodded. *Oh no, our work! Is Papa's work over? I'll have to find a job immediately.*

Pushing the ashtray aside, he leaned toward her and spoke quietly. "You must have noticed how our cases are drying up."

Magdalena wondered what that meant. "Do you mean you are out of money?"

Sciacca's smile was that of a father for a child. "No, my goddaughter, but you will have to think of closing the practice at the house."

More curious than ever, Magdalena looked perplexed. "What does that mean, Jimmy?"

Leaning farther across the table, Sciacca reached for her hand. "It means we are moving to Las Vegas, and I want you to do some work for us there, Counselor."

Printed in Great Britain
by Amazon